Sue Woolfe spen   of
New South Wale   ity
and the Universit   ..ns,
written textbooks and edited film subtitles.

She is the author of *Painted Woman* and *Leaning
Towards Infinity*, both novels and plays, and the editor of
the anthology, *Wild Minds: Stories of outsiders and dream-
ers*. With Kate Grenville she is co-author of *Making Stories:
How ten Australian novels were written*. She has a
daughter.

For my daughter

This book began when I heard that in the mid-1980s in Australia, a judge acquitted a man of the crime of murdering his wife in bed. In his summing up of the case, the judge explained his decision, saying that any man could do this at the moment of passion.

Today, acquittals like this are not uncommon.

ACKNOWLEDGEMENTS

While writing this book, I read Theodor Adorno's work on aesthetics, and Peter Fuller's; I also read Marion Miller's description of the process of learning to paint from the other-than-conscious mind, Rene Girard's suggested links between sacred rituals and the universal attempt to contain violence, and Rozsika Parker's and Griselda Pollock's discussion of women artists as social constructs. These texts informed, sometimes invaded mine; they became the soul of *Painted Woman*, or perhaps they already were her soul, because who knows when a beginning happens? For example, months after the first edition of *Painted Woman* was published, I came across a certain sentence in Michel Foucault (quoted by Margaret Coombs in *The Best Man For This Sort of Thing*). That sentence which I'd never read before, seemed to have been with me always.

I am also in debt to Eva Hesse, Andrew Brighton, William Wharton and Donald Kuspit for their writings on art, to artists Kerry Johns and my father Alex Edwards, to my agent Lyn Tranter, and to Gordon Graham, who urged me on and held the baby.

Contents

'From the idea that the self is not given to us, I think that there is only one practical consequence; we have to create ourselves as works of art.'

MICHEL FOUCAULT

'You must conduct *Tosca*, otherwise you might kill someone.'

HERBERT VON KARAJAN (in an interview)

Self Portrait One

Oil on plaster
10 ft x 12 ft, 12 ft x 14 ft,
8 ft x 10 ft, 18 ft x 8 ft

Oil on plywood
20 ft x 3 ft

Oil on laminex
6 ft x 4 ft

Oil on lino
12 ft x 18 ft

His arm is above me. I'm thinking that he may hit me the way he hits my mother, his face slashed between the red protuberances of nose and chin, his lips purple, his teeth flaring like a saw's edge. So I look down and align my feet the better for balance, and pull my skirt tightly over my crouched knees, because if I'm knocked over I must not show my panties.

Mum always falls decorously, if noisily.

Yesterday as the material of her dress shrieked in his hands, her silk panties, puckered at the waist by elastic, came into view.

He brings his arm down all in one movement, but the brush curves against the wall and flattens out leaving behind a trail of glossy blue. I breathe, allow my feet to be comfortably pigeon-toed. I'd run but the door's a long way off, the door handle's high, and he might not know I'm here wedged between two chairs.

His elbow snakes and the shining blue trail bends this way, that way, this way. He lifts the brush away from the wall, the bristles up to prevent drips, he pauses, and I straighten my feet again and knock my teeth on my knee. His brush is returning to the top curve, absorbed and now looping, twisting, all the way down the wall like smiles, and I want to laugh with them but that would give me away.

Now there's a blue silent shape on the white wall.

He dips the brush into the paint pot, deep down so the bristles are plump and blue, they come up streaming blue. He holds the brush inside the curving shape, and paints an A on its side. Then a half-circle above.

He backs away from the wall and stands at arm's length. A drip falls from his brush. His head's on one side.

I dodge the chair arm and tilt my head on one side too.

It's an eye, side-on. An eyebrow. Hair. A face in profile. A woman's long hair. My mother.

Now he begins again, this time higher up, vertical spikes side by side, then another flow down the wall, more angular this time, zig zag, and I see it's a second profile, jutting out where the first curved in: a big right angle, a nose, two lumps—that's a mouth—then the paint festers in bubbles as he loops up the wall again all the way to the vertical spikes. Another A on its side with a half-circle above. An eye looking at her eye. A man's face watching her face.

He stands back. I sink so close to the chair I can smell its ancient dust. He dips the brush into the pot again; and nudges it against the pot's sides. He lifts his arm and paints over the man's lips, pushing them forward, pushing, straining, as if they're reaching to suck. To kiss. The man's lips want to kiss the woman's. Maybe the man wants to kiss my mother.

But now he moves up the wall again, and paints above the woman's eye a big X, a big blue X. It's a bow, the woman's wearing a big blue bow like mine.

Then he turns, nudges the brush again to make the blue run off, just some of it, and he paints a huge circle around the man and the woman with the bow like mine, a circle that cuts them off from the wall as a knife could, so they'd no longer be held onto the wall, so they could drift out the window away from The Gap, The Gap would close behind them as paint quietly closes into itself in the pot when the brush has gone.

He drains the brush, lays it carefully across the top of the pot, wipes his hands on his trousers, comes towards me. He's looking at me, I can't pretend he isn't. I stand to take the blow but his lips are smiling, his eyes are smiling behind the paint-flecked glasses, and he sits on the chair with a plump and pulls me over the chair's arms. It hurts but he's kissing me, my father's lips are kissing me, pushing onto my lips, I'm tickled by the wrinkles on his lips and the whiskery parts of his jumper and the smell of turps and sweat on his skin but he holds me tight. There's no pain, only where the chair arm hit my shin, and we're curving into each other and he's laughing so I laugh too, light bouncing from him to me and back, and the knot in my stomach unties and I curve my arms around his neck and his warmth seeps into me. And after a while of shadowy warmth and relief and kissing I look back at the wall and me, and I'm strong with his arm around me, and not a tear shed for my mother.

There was always The Gap, I swear I knew about it right from the start. Oh, I see how you in the front row smile and twitch your toes, but I knew. From the moment I broke the first doll's head and found inside only a brand name. Budget Toys. Synthetic Rubber. When I saw the first Christmas present wrappings lying on the floor, emptied of hope. When I knew that arms holding me could fall away by a will that wasn't mine. When I saw the distance between the breast and me. The dreaded, awesome distance.

I didn't need philosophers to point it out, find names, say that it made sense, or nonsense. It was there. But if it was, so was a place where there was no Gap. A place incandescent with meaning.

And that, ladies and gentlemen, became my purpose. From the start. To find that place beyond The Gap, so it would close behind me.

There's always The Gap, that makes you tired behind your knees as you stare at the lumps of stone in the road.

Auntie says that tiredness is merely boredom. Boredom is a state of mind, that's all, and I'm never bored, says Auntie. She visits from the city not to chat but to inspect my mother, even her pink scalp peering up under thin hair as she sits down to afternoon tea.

There's always something to do, she says.

Mum and Dad spend a lot of time looking out windows, separately. I wonder if they know about The Gap. Now Mum fiddles with the last button on her cardigan, as if she might wrench it off and throw it whirling into the sky.

But is it worth doing? she murmurs.

Her lips vibrate so much I could swear there was another mouth beneath the one on top. But I can't talk to that other mouth. Everyone would say it isn't there.

Auntie's list of things to do:

learn to sit with your legs together

learn to say thank you prettily even if you're disappointed

learn to leave some tea at the bottom of the cup

learn how to get dirt from under your fingernails when no-one's looking and, when they are, look them back in the eye to show you've been thinking about them.

*

You have a shocking bruise on your arm, says Auntie to Mum.

Shocking. Did you fall?

Mum's hand moves the biscuit plate over a grease stain on the table-cloth.

Your brother, she tells Auntie hurriedly, is a very passionate man.

She looks around, as if, she didn't mean to say it.

I know, says Auntie. She doesn't understand Mum, I can tell, by the way her teeth squelch on an Iced Vo-Vo, jealously.

Often Dad paints nudes, who pose at our house, in his studio.

Beauty is all a woman needs, says Mum when Auntie has gone. Or so they taught me.

She bisects my scalp with a hairbrush.

It takes pains to be pretty, she explains.

Today's nude is walking down the garden path. She wears a green plastic raincoat. I can't tell if she's got anything on underneath.

She always sits for him on Wednesdays.

She's a beautiful woman, says Mum. I was too. So beautiful, your father couldn't wait to get his hands on me.

As the nude turns the corner of the house, there's a rainbow across her green shoulders, from one shoulder to the other, an arch. But it goes as she wrestles with an umbrella.

Did you pose for Dad? I ask Mum.

No! she laughs. She takes a breath to say more, but doesn't.

Dad's eyes move along the body of the nude as he paints at his easel near the three-mirrored dressing-table crammed with tubes, jars, tins, boards, drawing pins, rubbers, rags, pens, soft-leaded pencils, hard-leaded pencils, charcoal, a knife. He works on his toes, one leg concedes weight to the other, one trouser leg stretches and crinkles. He holds out his brush to measure the nude. The nude is three-quarters of a brush long. One of the mirrors swings on its hinges and the nude undulates like a wave.

Will you put on a heater? she asks.

There isn't one here. I'd have to go and look for one, says Dad.

Well, could you? Like, go and look for one?

The nude's breasts are large and small as the wave breaks and recedes. In front of the glass door of the grandfather clock, I put my sandals down my bodice. They've fallen too far. They're nearly at my waist. I jockey them up. The material strains, holds. It outlines only shoe straps and buckles. The grime on the soles grates against my chest. Even with eyes half-closed, there's The Gap.

I don't want to interrupt my work, says Dad to the nude. I'm already losing the light. Think yourself warm.

I stand on a pinnacle of rock that elevates me above the tangled undergrowth at the back of the house. The sky is grey, the bush is grey, below is a grey valley. It's worse at dusk in the bush. It's not just the grey sadness, although that's there too. It's the maddening sense that something is being withheld. Like the words Mum didn't say. The withholding silence. Even if I uncurled the fern frond, peeled the bark down, dug into the ant hill, scraped away the red mould, I wouldn't find what I want to know. Not that I know what it is.

There's no point shouting but anger rises in my throat.

Tell me! I shout in my head. Tell me!

Afterwards, Mum and I shell peas.

Love, says Mum, should mean everything to a woman.

Peas ping into the basin.

There'd been a strip of light under their door. The springs creaking under the black-and-white striped mattress. Then a floorboard. A thud, that hot sound of flesh on flesh. A scuffle of sheets or bodies or both. Another thud, or was I moving? Sweat trickling down my backbone, or has my blood gone yellow? Another thud. I wasn't moving then. I run squinting into the light. His hand is coming down against her face, fast, thrilling the air, the exultant clap, the jerk of the chin, she reels, is reeling, it's a mad, wonderful game, but she smells red with blood and her nightdress, discreetly buttoned, slips to show her breast in that ghastly white light, her sad, shameful breast, and I reel in her screams, that she should be so exposed, and when we fall down, I fall down with her, she falls on the folds of her nightdress and I pull it from under her weight and button it away from anyone's eyes, if anyone's here to see, and wipe the blood from her lips with my sleeve, where it dries, black.

After a while she gets up and says she's sleepy and goes back to bed, and all I can do is watch green birds fly past my window till breakfast time.

At breakfast I say: Tell me what's important.

She says she will, but all she tells me is how to poke the clothes boiling in the copper. I warm my hands in the rising steam but it only makes them clammy.

Love is all a woman has, says Mum as we peg the clothes out. Whatever else she's hoped for.

I hope you're proud of your father, says Auntie.

In her backyard in the city, the dirt smells of sadness. An earthworm struggles towards her spade.

He used to be famous, she says. Exhibitions every six

months, overseas galleries, prizes, trips to sixteen cities: La
Paz, Athens, Mysore, London, New York. Sixteen. He took
me on one. We were treated like royalty. He was the king,
I was the queen.

You were the queen? I ask. What of?

Him, she says.

I laugh in disbelief.

I made him wear ties to all the dos. He took a lot of
notice of me, says Auntie.

She leans on her spade. I lean on mine.

In those days, she adds. Before your mother.

She sees the earthworm, chops it in half.

Can't Mum help him now? I ask.

Ha! says Auntie.

We keep digging. Auntie works her way down to the
fence and back.

They say he's yet to do his greatest work, she says.

Does it matter? I ask. Isn't love everything?

She stops, pushes her glasses back up her nose to her
forehead. It makes her seem knowledgeable, this gesture. It
makes me wait for her answer.

Not to a man, she says. It's different for men. He looks
to God, a woman looks to God in him.

We don't plant anything in the holes.

There's a sound in the studio. Breathing. No, faster than
breath and more jagged. In the three-way mirror his head's
on his arms. Tins lean under his weight. A pencil's about
to roll off the dressing-table. He's crouched three times. I
struggle with the reality of it. It's so momentous, private.
Dad is weeping.

I creep away.

I'm swinging on the gate to the chook yard, swinging back

and forth, back and forth, with my body drifting in a hazy circle of singing hinges and straw and dirt and manure and the dandelions bending back and forth, back and forth, and there's no Gap now, just this circle on my sun-warmed arm as I swing time and dandelions sway.

Dad's at my side, suddenly.

His arms stick out from his waist and the points of his elbows perforate the sky and his hands are red axes. But he's my friend, who painted me in loops and curves and smiles.

Dad, I ask, making my mother's eyes, Dad, am I beautiful?

The whiskers in his nostrils flatten with his outbreath.

Is that all you can think of? he shouts. Just what your mother would ask.

There's no kiss in his voice now. The sky presses down on my head. The fences are overgrown with brambles. I think about the way my mother screams as she falls, a note held high so that as she collapses, the note waits in the air. Not even her scream belongs to Mum.

No, I say. I'm not like Mum.

But he's turning away, walking up the yard. I'm alone under the sky and I know I'm puny. And there's yawning desolation in the distance between him and me.

I make the trees race past, bobbing up and down, till I pant in front of him.

I'm not like Mum, I shout.

But I'm spread-eagled on his glasses. He pauses, snorts, walks around me. I watch him go, and then the words are there, because despair teaches.

Well, look, I'll make no bones about it, I'll tell you from the start what I really think. I've seen too much and I think violence is at the heart of everything. I don't just mean that we're violent. It is.

*

I don't want to ever be like Mum, I shout.

If something else grows in the silence of the night I'll cut it off, the way Mum prunes roses, lopping their gentle heads, to make the treasured part more treasured.

In his flashing panes of light I'm fierce, ugly, angular, red.

You know things. She doesn't know what you know, I shout. So I want to be like you.

She only knows about washing clothes, and love.

His hands rest on my shoulders. They rub the material of my dress against my skin. He crouches in front of me as if he were my size. I look only at his glasses. I see only myself in his glasses. I don't look at him.

I'll teach you how to be like me, he says.

My boots sink in the mud of the yard.

Mum stands at the mirror, brushing her hair, watching herself. She sighs as she brushes. She watches her sighs.

His violence is having a terrible effect on you, she says. I can see it in your face. It's already harsh. At six years old, your face is already harsh.

It doesn't matter what people look like, I say. It's what people know.

Words splinter time. There's the era before, and the era after, like the unrolling of the Red Sea. She's gazing at me as if she's seen me for the first time.

We'll go away, she says. Somewhere he can't follow.

No! I yell.

Auntie, visiting again, loves tragic men.

No matter how powerful they are, she says, you can sniff the tragedy. You can almost lick it off them.

She's wiping a plate with a painting on it of a bridge.

There's a poem I'm reminded of, says Auntie. A man's

daughter ran away from him, she tried to escape in a boat but she drowned.

> The waters wild
> Went o'er his child
> And he was left lamenting.
> My daughter, O, my daughter.

I watch the O of her mouth. O my daughter. My father's lips would make that same sad shape if I went away with Mum. O my daughter. I hurt with the pain he'd suffer.

Auntie almost married when she was young. A dentist, she said. But she was forced to disappoint him.

I had, she says, looking up to Dad's studio, other responsibilities then.

The dentist was a powerful man.

There wasn't a mouth in this town, she says, that didn't owe something to him.

I'm suddenly pleased to be wiping up with Auntie. We are both his queens.

Often I sit in my parents' gaunt dark wardrobe, for the brush of her dresses against my hot face. My mother is not a woman of grand dresses, but there's one dress that's long enough to touch my head as I crouch. It's all rustling pink and black checks that swing full-skirted towards my upturned head, puffed sleeves and a low dipping neck velvety with a black frill. My mother calls it her taffeta. She never wears it.

When will you wear that? I ask her one day when she discovers me in the wardrobe, and gently pulls me out.

She sighs, she always sighs.

I never did, she says.

She straightens the dress on its hanger, where it rustles companionably, as if it's confiding in her, as if it wants to be part of her. There's a puff of perfume in the air. Wear it now, I say, expecting her to agree, I'm daring her and her sadness.

To my surprise she takes off her jumper and slacks, and pulls the dress over her head. It finds its place immediately around her body. She turns to me, the skirt swirling, eager, her hair loose and swirling with it, her face alight. Suddenly she's my friend, almost my age.

Your father was going to a special evening in his honour. I bought it to wear that night, she says.

What night? I ask.

A long time ago, she says. Before you were born.

I imagine a ball, glamorous women dancing with gentle-men who bend their heads to hear the women's excited chatter, my mother starry-eyed and moving like a princess, holding the hem of the taffeta dress high so her tiny feet could leap under its swishes. I'm furious with my mother, that she refused the magic of this dress.

Why didn't you wear it? I ask. It's lovely! You should have worn it!

She's half-way through another turn, laughing at the swirl of the skirt, she's flaring into the light, she's almost made of light. But she catches sight of herself in the dressing table mirror. Perhaps it's that, or the anger in my voice. Suddenly she's yanking the dress off, forcing it onto its hanger, banging the wardrobe door shut, pulling on her ordinary clothes.

There's The Gap inside me again, I'm frantic to find the red-cheeked little girl in her face that was there for such a short time, the little girl who could be my friend. I manage to make my voice softer.

You were lovely just then, I say. I wish you'd worn it to the ball.

She looks down at the mat with its faded yellow roses.

I never went, she says.

You didn't go with my father! I protest. You should have gone with my father!

He didn't want me to, she says. He took someone else.

Auntie, I say. I'm shrill with my certainty. He would have taken Auntie.

He didn't take your aunt, she says.

You should have made him take you! I say. Fury is back in my voice, breaking it, fury at my mother's complicity with sadness.

I couldn't, she says.

Why not? I demand.

He took Wednesday's model, she says.

Nude? I ask, but she's gone from the room.

Dad begins to teach me what's important.

People don't stand on their toes, says Dad. Their feet come towards you. Larger and larger. They could engulf you. Then they recede. All things recede. And while they recede, they seem to come towards each other.

Things recede, says Dad, as you move. They go somewhere you can't.

It isn't true, says Dad. But that's how we see. People have seen in other ways, the way they believed the world to be. Nowadays we see ourselves separate from things. We're not. It's an illusion. Artists have taught this illusion.

Why doesn't someone complain? I ask.

An illusion, says Dad, enchants.

One moment the hen shed is boards and the smell of bran and eggs and corrugated iron and a rim of dandelions.

The next moment it looms wide at the front and narrow at the back, like an ancient pyramid on its side pointing silently to infinity.

One moment the house is inside and outside me.

The next moment the gutters shift and the foundations shift and the bricks change shape and the windows and doors change shape, they all loom towards me and recede. They recede towards the road and the road recedes to the town and the town to the mountains, they recede to the place where all things meet, but don't.

I stand close to Dad's body to smell sweat and turps and linseed oil, the smells of the master of illusion, who knows.

It becomes a game between us, to talk about illusions. I practise them, and save them up in my head, where they bustle.

Have you noticed how gently bark lies on the ground, he says.

How wet the sun is on leaves, I say.

There are pinnacles on the stones in the road, he says. And leaves rush out of stems as if pushed.

These days I stand at the studio window with him. I put my hands behind my back like he does. I make my knuckles white like his.

The paints lie on the palette in ritual order. In stillness they're pent up. Their names are like a chant: cadmium yellow, cerulean blue, alizarin crimson, viridian green, vermilion.

On such days I forget about The Gap.

On the other hand, Mum knows nothing. She chews food at the front of her mouth, dutifully. She cuts the chop into small pieces.

Chew each mouthful thirty-two times, she says. That way you'll have a flat stomach.

We chew.

You'll go to school when you and I settle down in our new home, she says. It's high time.

I speak through mush.

Dad wouldn't want me to leave him, I say. He's teaching me to be an artist.

If we stayed, he'd treat you like he's treated me, she says. You'd die. We have to leave.

There are tears in her eyes. I look at the meat on my fork. When she feels for her handkerchief I swallow the next mouthful fast, greedily, without chewing.

I've made a terrible wish. If I fit twenty faces onto one page of the special sketch book he gave me with grey marbled edges, my wish will come true.

When I ask him to sharpen the pencil it turns turns turns in his hand, his knife flicks away what's unnecessary, it lies dead on the floor, the whirling lead goes on to become a mountain, a spire, and his arms are deft with authority, a dozen arms, a god.

I'm on the ninth face, the faces full on.

Less nuances than a three-quarter face, he says, but it'll do for a start.

The start of my life as an artist. He says that I mustn't draw circles for faces but ovals, like eggs. And take the line right back to where I began because there's no open part in the head to peer into, it's closed, secret.

I draw another nine ovals and run out of space, but that means she'll still be alive when I go into their bedroom to check. A spell is a serious matter.

We must respect the images of the past, Dad says. We see only because of the way they saw. Seeing is cumulative.

Today he shows me how to make the ovals into faces. We bisect the faces as if we're using an axe. A vertical line half-way across. Then a horizontal. The nostrils and mouth on the vertical. The eyes on the horizontal. Gashes for eyes, nostrils, lips. The gash for the lips just a little longer.

The axe head was comfortingly shiny the day before Christmas, the hen's neck thrust at the air, the dust was untidy in the air, and no pencil could have closed that circle.

This is the house where Dad and I will live when my wish comes true. Here's the sun coming out the chimney, and the music in the garden. I make the curtains and sing and the stitches are tiny and the iron leaves no creases. And only the smell of hot sweet cakes baking, and the turps and sweat and linseed oil. Here's the cat coiled in peace, in warm earth colours, burnt sienna, yellow ochre, burnt umber, just dark blue in the shadows because cats uncoil. And here's our bed, the bed I will share with my father, the valley from his body, the hill, and the valley from mine, and we walk over the hill to kiss and say goodnight and to kiss and say good morning. There's no darkness in this house, even the nights glow.

We lie side by side under the apricot tree. He tells me to look at the sky between the boughs. He puts his hand over mine.

And my hand is in a tent out of the wind and full of warmth. I lie back and look wherever he says. For a while there are only boughs rubbing against the sky, but the space of the sky extends to the edges of my mind, framed by boughs, the sky is pinned down by boughs as my father's canvases are pinned, or else it would go on and on, limit-less. My father has painted the sky his canvas with blue, the fire of cobalt blue, and now I have eyes all over my body to see the fire from my father, eyes on my neck and hands and thighs and in the spaces between my ribs, cobalt blue eyes seeing my father's sky and my father's sky seeing me. I am alight in the fire.

It's not the flower itself we paint, he's saying. It's the feeling of the flower.

The flower's so close it's two flowers and four and one, and he's so close I could eat it with his mouth.

You must see without looking, he says. You must sense.

The sky has paled to white with my straining.

Don't you feel the colour, its heat, on your face? he asks.

I want to, I want to, but no-one has told me before. Mum hasn't prepared me at all.

He flicks the flower away. It shivers on the grass.

I lie face down in the warmth where he was. I was in a tent with him, I could have lived in it forever if Mum had been a proper mother.

I stride towards the studio door, the way he strides. I dawdle there, to find a sentence.

Come in. I've drawn you, he calls.

Even across the room, his knuckles are sharp. His front tooth is broken and may cut his underlip.

It is, he says, a warning.

I could go back into the garden, the door behind me is still open. But there's a moment only now and then that sparkles. I walk towards that moment.

At first the portrait is all slashes, as if the canvas had been struck. But he wants me to know, his hands grasp my shoulders to make me know, and I see irregular, shadowy, familiar, a face.

Just like you, he says.

It's my mother.

Your mother, he says, stops me from finding my own

bright possibilities, from finding what's inevitable in me. She cloys me. She's always so miserable.

I'm staring into the dark places of my father's mouth, and his sketch, and the creases of his body.

Although I don't know what cloy means, I say: She cloys me too.

There was a moment, a particular moment, when I fell under a spell, I became enchanted, in that less familiar sense of the word. Enchanted, though it's hard to pin down exactly what with. It could've been my father's anger exploding out in the paint. Or the way the painting contained his anger. Or the movement between the two, the tension between the art and the violence, and the exhilaration that burst out of a painting still as a stone, just propped there against an easel.

I've painted that moment, see, down here, it's like an old Greek carving of Pegasus flying out of the blood of Medusa, and up into the sky.

I stare into those dark places and become as clean as if I'd gone into Dad's sky and as clear, with all the despair burnt away. So now I can tell my wish. I've wished my mother dead.

These brush strokes are my mother's hair.

She sighs so much, my mother, when I touch her hand or brush her long wavy hair, she sighs into her teacup and the china stretches thin with helplessness. These days she doesn't change out of her nightdress, even for Auntie's visits. But Auntie whispers to get her back on the right track:

How to get rid of stains: You've got to get the mixture perfect, that's the secret, mix it to a paste with warm water, test it, and you only need enough to fill a hollow tooth, if you use too much it eats the fabric. I heard a woman on the bus, she was talking about her niece, her niece had used the wrong proportions, she wasn't a careful girl, and there she was, standing in Woolies, and the elastic in her panties went.

Mum belches behind a sad hand, a snail's trail of saliva on her wedding ring. Auntie waves goodbye encouragingly but her stockings wrinkle around her heels.

Mum sees the wrinkles too.

We'll be out of this soon, says Mum to me. Soon.

But Dad's brush, Dad's eye pulls boldly at the mystery. He's always there, even when I walk in the late afternoon sun, there he is in my mind. The apricot tree has lost the day's warmth. I sit on the side away from the house. The mountains have drained the sky of colours.

But his eye is a glittering transparency in profile fixed on the canvas, his brush feels for the whorls of colour on the palette, he knows their exact colour and formation.

I know what his paintings are about, she sighs.

Does he think of me as he reaches out to the lines that are real but aren't, that meet but don't, to that point where everything shifts? At that moment, if I looked, if I knew the exact moment, if I knew exactly how to look, I'd be able to reach out too.

I'm trying to go where no-one else has gone, he says.

Does he wish it was me when she stands there, offers him a pot of tea he doesn't want, comments he doesn't want, twisting cream into her hands?

You don't help him find his possibilities, I tell her.

You might as well put down your handbags and coats, please don't hang anything on the easel, take your time, there's a whole story in the paintings if you care to put the pieces together for yourselves.

Sometimes when there's been peace between them for a while and the house is quiet with morning and only a bough scraping on the gutter, he makes her a cup of tea.

The kettle echoing with the gush of water. The click of the cupboard door. The cold scrape of china. The puff of gas in the pipes. I stand watching.

He sees me watching, begins to hum, I'm still watching, he holds the kettle high above the teapot, pouring slowly, he lowers it smoothly down its own shining stream.

He puts the pieces of bread in the toaster, one on each side, careful of crumbs. He leans on the working-board, watches the element glow red. I come into the kitchen, lean on the working-board too. But he's humming, the humming becomes a song, there's no space for explanations, he flings open a door of the toaster, plucks out toast, throws it onto a plate, flings open the other door, plucks out the other piece, throws it on top of the first. Singing many words. He gets the butter from the fridge and the milk, closes the fridge with his foot, spreads butter, pours milk, cuts toast, pours tea, singing.

I search the words of the song.

> But you'll look sweet
> Upon the seat
> Of a bicycle built for two.

He's taking the plate of buttered toast in one hand and the cup of tea in the other and walking up the hall to their bedroom, he's pushing open the door with his elbow and there's Mum, peaceful in a green shining nightgown, stroked by the early sun, steam rising white from the tea, her breasts rising for him, feet pointed that the bones might break to please him, to capture him, for after all he leaps across mountains in words and paint. As long as there are long shiny mornings sometimes, as long as he's a god, that's all that matters. Surely my mother knows this. In none of the stories must the gods be kind.

In the night, that night, there was a deep silence. It woke me. Not a cry, not a slap, not a creak. Just sharp, deep silence.

This is her body next morning. Not shiny but palely freckled and, under the white cotton sheet, held out by bones like a covered bird cage.

I sit beside her in the darkened room, scraping my chair on the floor, but there's no-one to reprimand the noise in that hush.

I examine her profile.

I've drawn hundreds of profiles in the last few days and found them to be, as Dad says, merely a matter of properly placed curves of different lengths and directions. But Mum's isn't.

Wasn't.

I wish he was here so I could show him. She has a convex curving forehead, and there's a small indentation slanting towards her eye sockets, but then there's a straight line, jutting way way out, a fierce nose, and a firm line from nose to upper lip. Almost as if she'd been cut out with scissors. Then there's another short straight line from lower lip to the top of the chin and only after that, curves, all the way to the sheet.

This morning I saw she was as still as the room. I put my ear to the steel bed frame, then against her side. All I hear is a spring in the mattress. Chunk. Like something you're trying to remember. Chunk. I ask her to open her mouth, and when she doesn't, I prise it open and push it shut. Like a door. I open her eyes and we stare at each other. My voice echoes in the hollows of her face. But she's staring me out, so in the end I flip her eyelids shut.

I wasn't sure I could do it, I tell her. But I have. And now it's done.

There's a green pen beside the bed and her diary, and since she won't want that any more, I open it and turn a few pages in and draw her profile again and again. A breeze rattles the window panes. In the hall, the grandfather clock chimes. The pen starts to go in the right directions. The sun spears through the slats in the blinds.

After a while, a car brakes outside.

She can't come back to you, says Auntie, arriving important in a taxi.

There's no point in sitting there waiting. I know you can see her on the bed, but she's not there. She's gone. Gone away. Gone away to heaven. And that's a far far better place for her to be.

It's hard to admit this, but I've had to admit many things and this is just one more: violence, in its terror, once seemed to me not just a simple means to an end, but behind that, a realisation of what is. The discovery of a secret.

Over here is the Athenian queen who had two drops of blood from the Gorgon. See, this one, it kills.

And this one, it nourishes life.

Because it seems to me now that violence can be both: it can be death and it can be, ladies and gentlemen, what you see around you in this room.

They're having trouble manoeuvring her, she's so still. And the red glass flowers on elegant stems in the door panels curve towards the stiff white sheet. Perhaps he told her how she would die. With my help. Perhaps they both knew about my magic. Perhaps she told him. There was no violence, I saw. I looked into their room in the silver night. No turning, turning, falling to the floor. Just silence. Only the rustle of the sheet, like insects in the undergrowth. The sheet that's now so still.

Here's the men marching with my mother's body. How carefully they carry her between the stained-glass door panels.

And Auntie behind the stained-glass flowers, a bead of water on the end of her nose. The bead gets bigger, drops on its own weight, a line shimmering down to the carpet in the stillness of the hall, she mops her nose with a screwed-up handkerchief as she speaks on the phone, but now the shimmering line joins the handkerchief to the carpet.

He is, she says into the phone, a gentle man. Passionate, of course, as artists are. But gentle. It must've been an accident.

No-one can see the shimmering line but me.

I'm sent to live with Auntie again. It's as dreary as the dust in the backyard. As still. As still as Mum's body. I swing on the gate with a newly laid egg in my hand and I'm swinging against the dandelions, against time, as if in the geometry of the circle I could close The Gap. The Gap is all around me. Dad has been taken away.

These days I'm always thinking about the destruction inside things, that everything seems to hold its paradox inside itself, suspended, immanent, waiting. See the tranquil scene, see how the paint holds back, restrains, there's violence inside, the paint trembles, the violence will break out in its own time—now, no, not now—you walk away, walk back, the scene is still so tranquil but you look back again, just to make sure. You say, how tranquil.

*

There are many lunches alone with Auntie. We eat other meals but breakfasts are foolish with hope and after dinner we sleep. But lunch begins the long afternoons. I chew many times, more than thirty-two times, many bites, many chews, so that the sun will move in the sky and Dad will return.

Sixteen teaspoons laid out on sixteen cups and saucers and each teaspoon with the name of the cities where Dad triumphed: La Paz Göteborg Graz Athens Fort Worth Birmingham Hyderabad Rome Bulawayo Malaga Reykjavik Wewak London New York Mysore Perth.

Triangular sandwiches of white bread with pink ham and white fat spilling out. A sponge cake with jam smears on the side. A sherry decanter with a chip in the glass ball on the top. Auntie with a black bow hat on her thin hair and no spectacles doesn't notice a moth's wing trapped between the lid and the bottle. Then she has to blow it away surreptitiously when she does the honours.

And talk. Who's going to eat all this food it was only an accident he might get life it was only an accident a good thing he confessed straightaway did you hear he went crazy when he realised what he'd done only an accident you can see in his paintings what a gentle soul.

No-one sees me. Only Auntie speaks about Mum.

A shame hardly anyone came, Auntie says. On such an important day for her.

Your father went crazy when he realised what he'd done, says Auntie. He wouldn't hurt a fly. He takes pity on everyone. Everything. I've never known anyone so full of . . .

We're washing cups. We stare at the mountains. We keep examining the mountains until we have to look where to put the cups.

... so full of fellow feeling, says Auntie.

We balance sixteen cups carefully against each other.

Your father's a great man, says Auntie. A man of genius. Men of genius need a lot of understanding. And no-one has ever understood him. Except me.

And me, I say, but she doesn't hear.

We wait in the stillness, Auntie and I, listening to each other walk on the floorboards, in the spring chill. Sometimes we warm our hands around cups of tea as friends do. Every day her skin stretches more between her cheekbones and jaw as if something drags at it. While the tea glows amber in the white cups.

You might have to do these things for your father, says Auntie. Now your mother's gone.

We're washing sheets. We drag a sheet flowing with water from the grey concrete laundry tub.

Water runs down my sleeves. She pushes the sleeves hard up my arm so that I shiver, but not with the damp.

I may not be asked to live with you, she says.

She hands me a corner of the sheet. The cloth is clammy against my skin.

Your father and I used to be like that, she says.

Her fingers pressed together are ancient with water. Her eyes search mine, as if I could offer something. Then her fingers fly apart. We twist the sheet together. We watch the water running into the drain, but I'm thinking about her eyes. The twists approach my end thick and angry, the sheet writhes in my fingers, leaps out. She bends down, picks it up, pushes it back into my hand. As if I've taken something.

But at the line, we flap the sheet like angels.

I did everything for your father, she says.

Soothed by memories, she pegs sheets gently. I hand the

pegs. She goes to prop up the line. Her shoes are trodden down at the heels and her hips without a corset bulge.

What did you do for Dad? I call after her, shading my eyes in disbelief.

When we were kids? She pulls at the cross bar.

Everything. Everything, she says.

She spreads out red hands and I suspect she might claim that even the purple mountains leaning against the sky were her cut-outs. She comes back and picks up the washing basket and holds it against her waist so that her body curves around it and then I can concede that she might have once been young.

Your father has always been passionate, she says. As your mother used to put it. What she didn't appreciate is that he needed a lot of protecting.

Something in her tone heats my blood in such a rush I want to pee. I stand hot in the clear cold spring sunlight.

What from? I demand.

She smiles, her smile stops and the lines on her cheeks are as knowing as thorns.

Himself, she says.

She turns and walks back to the laundry. But there's nothing there when I look. Only puddles on the cement floor.

Auntie listens to news commentaries about Fidel Castro.

Good-o, she says to the radio. Good-o.

How did my mother die? I ask.

She turns the volume down.

No-one's done anything wrong, she says. She pauses. Swallows, as if she's trying to force stones down her throat.

Castro's talking now, she says.

She turns the volume up.

*

So now I know we both did it, Dad and I, together we did this awesome thing, and I jump between the sunshine and the shadows and touch the petals of the wild bush flowers that spray pollen at me. Dad and I together, it's much more awesome than doing it by myself, it makes us one person. And that means I'll never again feel that nothing in the universe cares whether I move this finger, this toe, this hand, this foot. Or whether I don't. Never again feel that nothing matters, that nothing is neither important nor unimportant, just indifferent. Never again hope to dissolve into the horizon, that blur between sleep and death, not sweet like sleep, not absolute like death, just a dissolving into The Gap. Because if we can do this together, if I'm so much part of him, then I'll be part of him when he pulls at the mystery, I'll be there, I'll know what he knows, Dad will escort me into meaning.

If only he would come home.

He strides across the garden, a painting in each hand. His arm swings out and I can almost see one of the pictures. I think I see. But afterwards, I can remember nothing. Only the creasing of his trousers around the knee cap, and one of his shoelaces flopping untied. And my straining to see, the knowledge that this moment is very important, that I must concentrate, remember. Although all he's doing is walking across the lawn with paintings. It's his stride, it's the days of silence since his return, it's the tent of other paintings on the lawn, the saucepan of soup steaming behind me on the stove, the care with which he props the paintings against each other, the meticulous care, that warn. And yet with all these warnings, all I can call to mind afterwards in detail are wrinkling trousers and a flopping shoelace. Not the details of the paintings.

Are they his paintings? I ask.

What do you mean? asks Auntie.

For a moment the sun whirls along the tops of the paint-ings like a halo but slips away and there's all the dark night ahead. Dad walks back across the garden, back to his studio, and the pale shapes float on the grey lawn and a scissor-beaked crow cries from the fence. Now he comes out again with two more paintings, but halfway across he stops, turns, heads towards us. I slip down from the window.

Set the table, says Auntie, who's also been watching.

The cutlery drawer is warm brown wood and the felt under the cutlery is a green fur that presses back gently against my fingers as Dad whips the walls of the house so the clay masks he made jump on the walls. Slashing, and words too loud to understand, and perhaps the walls will come down and the trembling lightshade will fall into the soup. And now a hoarse creaking and something, many things, are being wrenched apart, but Auntie walks back to the stove and stirs the soup and she's rounded with steam.

The bush is dark between our house and the township where there are lights and people drinking tea and chatting.

Will he kill us? I ask but under the hammering and break-ing my voice is a whisper. Another smash. The fridge leaps into life. The steam from the soup wafts between my legs and leaves them moist. And Auntie's hungry eyes on me, it's a look of hers that I remember. His footsteps crunch. He's very close to us. Now he's ripping something, some-thing that shrieks in his hands.

Finish setting the table, says Auntie in her usual voice but her lips don't go back to their usual place over her teeth. So I count the knives and forks and spoons quickly, the faster to turn around and see that all there is behind me is a pot of soup and her face.

Then I get his tray with the doily that Mum embroidered

with crosses and I lay the spoon and fork and knife parallel and Auntie comes over and straightens a corner.

My mother doing cross-stitches on doilies, pricking her fingers in the late afternoon because Dad hadn't had all that success just to throw away money on electricity bills, my mother bowing towards the window light, quiet on the worn velveteen love seat, stitching crosses on doilies, crosses of kisses or abnegation.

The hammering and smashing starts again, and now a clay mask does fall off the shelf and smash on the lino but in the shouting and wrenching, a smash is only a whisper.

I'll get the broom and dustpan, says Auntie.

I'll come with you, I say.

So we walk together through the rooms, switching lights on all the way and not switching them off on the way back, and outside the black night strains. I hold the dustpan on a slant while she sweeps and I look under the kitchen table for any missed chips and she gazes at the floor, the saucepan of soup, the walls, but not at the windows. We lift down the other masks.

The kitchen wall wasn't the place for them anyway, says Auntie. Several times I've had to take to them with the bottle washer.

She hands the masks to me one by one and I put them in the middle of the table in case the earth trembles again.

Neatly, says Auntie.

The earth does tremble again, more urgently than before, and Dad yelling bastard bastard bastard and the walls shaking and the best cups rattling, bastard bastard bastard.

Those broken bits, says Auntie, get some newspaper to wrap them up. Not the front page, she says as I grab it, the middle section, the TV section, the TV guide, you know what your father thinks of TV, all optics no examination that's what he thinks, he won't be wanting the TV guide, she gabbles.

In the black gunpowder night, paintings begin to explode.

Mum stitching those crosses as if they mattered, all those afternoons, while I sketched the profiles of her death. Then the white sheet so stiff between the stained-glass panels, the panels full of red flowers, the sheet so unadorned.

The grass crunches again, the spiky lawn. The night waits. I hear Auntie's heart but there's a beat behind it that might be his. A match scratches and a flame spurts and leaps on the window pane. Auntie grabs me as I run.

No, she says. Her voice hisses. While the nightmare twists on the glass.

No, she's saying, she might be shouting or whispering, I'm not sure. Her face is close to mine, her eyes quiver in certainty.

There are some things best not seen, she says.

Her lips smack together. The fire crackles and consumes. It's a while before she says what her lips have locked away.

And if you do see them, they're best not said.

She lets my hands drop. They fall to my sides as if they've never been there before. All around outside the fire screams.

Bastard, bastard. His voice as terrible as the night. And then there's a slop of kerosine and a whoosh as the paintings finally soar into the sky and now he's laughing louder than the fire.

And here, see, down here in the corner, here's my Aunt showing me how to cut parsley into tiny pieces, telling me not to breathe on it or it will blow away. While paintings burn.

I'm washing my hands in the bathroom, making the soap into gloves, and washing them off and making new gloves all the way up to my elbows, when the door handle turns and Dad's there. His face is touched with black, a mad clown's rouge, and there are black marks on his clothes and as he comes towards me he holds up his hand, his right hand, and the skin is puffy and purple against the white porcelain. It twists like a painting twists in searing heat, and then it hangs, a helpless sagging, a lump of flesh that could sag, jabbed by the dark hook in a butcher's shop. As it comes closer to me I see the purple skin ballooning with yellow air that must escape. I edge along the length of the bath, the lather drawing the skin on my arms.

I look into Dad's eyes, the first time I've done that since before we killed Mum together, and I see but I don't, and I know, but I don't.

We stand facing each other. I'm in white gloves I could flaunt at a ball, white as smiling, white as a beginning, and he has an animal hand. The ashes from paintings float in the sky between us like hawks. But I look down at the squares of lino on the bathroom floor, that go so evenly around the basin and the bath Auntie cleans every day. Though my voice is not quite mine, the words are clear.

The soup will be ready by now.

I turn without looking at him to the big white rectangle of the bath, much more real and solid than the night, and run the tap there so he can use the tap in the basin. The water runs louder than speech. My gloves come off but it's as if they're still on amongst chatter and clinking glasses and laughter and when I go out I look back and see that Dad's buttocks rest easily on his legs.

So I walk back to the kitchen, to the steam and Auntie's face, and she has taken off her glasses because they're useless in all that steam, and her eyes are exhausted, like someone who's looked too hard, and shouldn't.

Then I carry the tray with its doily of crosses through the echoing house to the little table set up outside his studio and I put the glass of wine over the spot that sloshed and make sure the knife and fork and spoon are parallel and the cheese is smooth in its dish and the parsley swirls easily on the shining surface of the soup. I knock three times on the door as Auntie has instructed and go away, not hiding around the corner to see, straight back into the dining room, and sit in front of my dinner.

So I don't speak to him. To know is enough. To know we killed her together. I willed it, he took the blame, but we did it together. One day he'll look me full in the face and he'll say it. He'll say: You know why it happened.

Yes, I'll say. I know.

Beauty, says Dad, is the hopeless attempt to break the spell of reality. It's the hopelessness that's beautiful.

He's painting the stillness of eggs, their warm brown smell when I lift them from the nest, but he paints white light trapped and turning inside them. The eggs are earth colours, umber and sienna in a green dish, and I float on the shine of the oils and he floats in his mind. He looks up at the windows, then down, and with a sudden stroke on the canvas he's trapped the blue shadows in the window frame, he's pushing them into the green dish and tucking them around the still eggs, we're anchored with them, but so still we may break free. And now he paints a yellow light that tugs at the eggs so they move and take up more space.

He puts his brush down in the indentation in his easel.

Do you know what I did to your mother?

I stare at the eggs. I blink so fast they're large and small. Large and small.

What did I do? Tell me, he says.

Large and small. And the wall, large and small. And my hand.

What, What, What, he says.

The words run into each other.

But I know this isn't the moment. The moment won't be like this.

Look at me, he says.

Looking is difficult, I used to find, you may find too. Sometimes when I raised my head to look there was a rushing of air, time changing speed, a semi-circle of dread. In case, in case. But there'd only be a person pre-occupied with something else. While a clock in my head still ticked loudly. In case, in case. Until the blessed blessed lowering of the eyes.

She died in the night, I say to him.

The heat fading from my face.

What I did, he's shouting. Not when it happened. What I did.

I raise my eyes as far as the eggs, lying complacently against each other in the green dish with the blue shadows. And then as far as his arms which he re-crosses. He shelters his hands in the folds of his jumper, and the simplicity of the gesture, the nudging of the hand against the clumsy wool, the hand wanting warmth, shelter, makes something go hard and bright in me. I've seen, known, not said. I'm as strong as he is, stronger. Why should I let him make me blurt out those details, so appallingly petty, he knows them, he knows as well the grandeur of our deed. What was that awesome death about if it wasn't to make us one? And he will acknowledge that, I will wait, I can wait longer, I shall endure.

Mum went to heaven, I say. And that's a better place to be.

She's lying in the cold ground, he says.

His lips leap with spit.

Rotting. Like a leaf, he says.

He's letting the night in, he's wilfully letting the chaos come screaming in. But I won't allow it.

She's not like a leaf, I say. So she's not rotting.

We stare at each other and he hates my strength. Whatever I'll feel tomorrow, right now the tears dry on my face. I'm tall, stretched out between the floor and the ceiling and the moment stretches like my body.

Then he looks down. He rubs his nose. He reaches for his glasses folded beside his easel. He puts them on, eases them over his ears. He rubs his nose again. He picks up the brush. He stands poised at arm's length from the canvas, and his shoulders and back ripple as he paints his signature in the corner. It takes a while to sign his name. Geoffrey Montrose. He steps back, almost collides with me. He looks me up and down as if he's surprised to see me here. Then he goes back to his easel, lays down his brush, takes the rag stopper out of the clean fresh smell of turps, wipes the paint off his hands.

It's time you started school, he says.

He turns back to the eggs drowning in colour.

I'm exhausted by ambiguity. Always the ocean of meaning under the tiny buoy bobbing in the sunshine. The galaxy in front of the telescope. So if I explain too much about my paintings, consider it a kindness. I've saved you from having to subordinate yourselves, like worshippers, to them, hoping they'll speak to you.

In this part of the painting is the smell of schooldays—

orange peel and vegemite sandwiches and wet raincoats.

The teacher hands out crayons, not oils that tremble into innuendoes, but with leads as unflinching as her teeth, which she sucks when no-one is looking. I look as she walks by because I'm two years older than the others, but she ignores me.

The small boy on my right grabs the black crayon as if it's a dagger. The lead breaks, the paper rips.

I want you to draw your home, says the teacher. Your home, she repeats so I suspect there's a secret locked inside words for her as well.

The boy ducks his head to listen to the whisper of another boy across the row. His cheeks bounce. But I've smiled too much today and my upper lip is ticking. In the playground cold with early morning sun, I smiled amongst the others. I pulled in my knees like they did, brushed the hair unnecessarily out of my eyes, rested my schoolbag between my legs. No-one noticed. At lunchtime under the peppercorn trees, sandwiches were exchanged, but not with me. Then I became more obsequious, and offered to turn the skipping rope.

What's your name? asked a blonde girl when she had cheated twice and my arms were wheels turning.

That was when the tic started. She went to report to the others. I kept turning the rope, though less certainly. The sunlit asphalt became black crumbs. The girls stood on them with perfect balance. The skipping rope floundered. A girl with red hair tidied into a blue bow came over.

Your mother's dead, she accused.

I examined her voice.

Yes, I said.

She took the rope, wound it up and went away. Her friends kept staring. I straightened my shoulders and stared back but my bowels were churning.

The cheeks of the small boy in my class are jumping on the red skipping rope of his lips. Nevertheless I draw shapes in the air above the paper like Dad does when he's planning a painting. The house will be two-thirds of the way down, a small shape among big mountains. The house will be purple and blue like fear. And here's an oval face yellow in the light but blue in the shadows. A three-quarters face looking out of the picture to somewhere past my shoulder.

The little boy nudges me. I pretend not to notice.

No. This will be the house here, a square on the side of a triangular mountain. This will be a woman wrenching off the roof. A triangular mountain, a square house, a triangular roof. And the woman will be in straight lines like bones. A woman with no flesh holding a roof over her head. She'll throw it while I run down the mountain under its shadow until it lands on me.

I know, says the little boy, looking at me.

I know who you are, he repeats.

He laughs behind a curved hand.

No. There'll be a house here bigger than any mountain, with a lid for a roof. There's a woman of bones bigger than any house. She holds the bones of her arms above her head and throws the lid of the roof which is bigger than any woman. But I'm running up the hill and the lid falls short because I'm bigger and faster.

I know, says the little boy.

His cheeks turn on the rope.

About your father.

The boy across at the other desk explodes with laughter.

He's a murderer, says the little boy.

His orange crayon screeches from one corner of the paper to the other, now across, down, across, across, across. The lead breaks. He breathes. Now the green crayon, zig zag.

Your father's a murderer. He laughs.

I hold the black crayon but wait until I find the black inside me, but as it rushes out it's so voluptuous I feel its taste, smell, the space it takes up, I'm dragging out more blackness as it drags at me, that night when secrets and bones collided, the stench of it, the rotting.

She's rotting like a leaf. I put her there to rot, Dad put her there to rot, but there was a reason, an awesome reason. All right, I'm evil and Dad's evil, we're evil together.

With the teacher's crayons, I draw the murder of my mother. Dad and me, murdering Mum.

Take it home to show your parents, says the teacher with unflinching teeth.

I dare not throw it away. Auntie's tidiness strips me bare.

I must wait.

How was school? Auntie slices the skin off a pineapple. Whole chunks of it fall away.

Good, I say. To end the conversation.

Now the pineapple is a thin pale thing. She hands me a slice. I eat carefully for fear of prickles.

Nothing has been said about my drawing, and I'm carrying the plates from the dinner table. The fat congeals.

If I make it to bedtime it'll be all right. Tomorrow I'll take the drawing back to school and tear it into strips to throw in the garbage tin with a lid that clangs shut. I stay so long in the bath my toes wrinkle.

My father is waiting for me in the bedroom.

How dare you! he shouts.

At first it's the force of a particular palm and particular fingers on particular bone, on this stretch of skin, then this stretch, and each blow is a new jolt that could make my skeleton leap out, and between each is a measured pause. But then the shocks become continuous, merging, so the searing from the last dulls the searing of the next, and if he keeps to this rhythm I might become accustomed to it.

Get out, shouts Dad to Auntie at the door.

His arm stays in the air.

I see my drawing in her hand. The pale gleam in her eyes. And the look that passes between her and Dad.

Here in the painting is my Aunt's life, the way she spent it, see here where the brush almost breaks free of the canvas, but stays, then comes away, too late.

But now the blows come questioningly, like prayers, each with passion but an uncertainty between, until this also becomes a ritual, so when I lie face down on the bed alone I can still hear that red grinding.

I become addicted to the grandeur of horror. When he locks himself away in the studio for weeks, I search my face for signs that I'm a killer. Those yellow grey marks under the eyelid, they weren't there before. Like an excrescence working its way through the skin, the bad in me coming out. And when I see him walking under the trees, that solitary step as if he's not treading on real ground but in the landscape of his mind, when he turns into the sun's last rays, I strain to examine his face. Those same yellow grey marks.

There are newspaper clippings under her wardrobe, and a board with sharp edges and her ball dress. When I hold it up in the gloom, its pink and black checks jostle, it swishes like a memory. But on the V-front, just where she would've smelt of soap and perfume and heat, a ticket has been stapled. I smell the sting of dry-cleaning spirit. Auntie has had Mum's dress dry-cleaned when she anaesthetised my parent's bedroom. And when I put the dress back in its place, the bones in the bodice protrude, like the sad carcass of a chook on the kitchen table at Christmas.

I don't look at the newspaper clippings or the board under the wardrobe. I push them to the back. They too have their own time, as meaning has.

After he'd hit me I'd woken to find next to my face a plate of buttered toast cut so fine it crumbled, and beyond, a cup steaming with milky tea. Dad warm and firm sitting on the bed's edge so the mattress slanted down to meet him. He'd been there always, it seemed.

Hurry up, he'd said. We're going to the city.

He went out. My leg was bruised. It hurt to turn towards the toast. Shadows of leaves shifted on the counterpane. Auntie came in with my best dress. She laid it smoothly over the arm of a chair.

Hurry up, she said. Don't keep your father waiting.

Isn't he angry any more? I asked.

She pushed her glasses against her forehead.

There are some things best not said.

The butter glittered on the toast.

We carve through the mountains to the city, Dad and I in the train, while the whistle shrieks. He holds my hand till it's sticky with sweat but I don't take it away. He shuts his eyes to the train's rhythm. At Parramatta he wakes up and offers me an ice-cream from the station vendor. I consider the chocolate topping and my best dress.

I don't know, I say.

He slams the window down and doesn't give me back his hand until we're at Central.

The station is so grand that the footsteps of the crowd

whisper. The roof falls into the round sky and hazes above us so anything might exist beyond. A man demands tickets. Above our heads a purple drop from a bunch of grapes jerks along the length of a neon sign and falls jubilantly into the outline of a wineglass.

Of course I bought tickets, Dad says to the guard. But I must have tossed them away. However, I can recall their colour exactly, if that will help—Winsor and Newton, Cobalt Turquoise 078 S4. Or if you'd prefer, on Rembrandt's chart they'd be Hooker's Green 044 P1.

Another drop of grape juice falls but the level in the wineglass doesn't rise.

Come on, says Dad to me.

He pulls my arm and we run into the crowd.

We're in a little lattice cage of a lift.

What floor, sir? asks a woman I hadn't noticed, although she's painted her lips vermilion for authority. Her hand is over a column of buttons.

I'm sure you know, says Dad. I am the artist.

He tips his body against the back wall. I do the same.

No-one told me we sold paintings.

The vermilion lips stay stretched. She looks at Dad through half-closed eyes. He stares past her at the closed door. There's a knocking from outside. The knocking gets louder. The woman presses a button and the door leaps open. Three women come in, one wheeling a pram.

Zippers, says the woman with the pram.

Thank you, says the woman with vermilion lips.

Make room, sir, she says to Dad. After all, there is a baby.

He doesn't move. I wonder if I should nudge him.

We're in a hurry, says the woman with the pram to the lift driver.

The door slams shut. Dad's lips are curving slightly upwards.

The woman finds our floor.

As we walk out of the lift I see a portrait of my mother.

I've only given you a few glimpses of my mother, the way she'd stand at a mirror with a brush, the way she'd lean across a table, so you'd see her the way I did then, as an obstacle between me and that perfect place where there was no despair. I couldn't have shown you the totality of her, I never knew it, but I could've hinted there was more, that she'd mastered the intricacies of ancient Greek, if she had, or that she'd been living for years in the Highlands of New Guinea studying the ways of food-gathering in a particular tribe. All I've shown, and all I know, is how she existed in the story I've lived, and I see now that I've lived that story for no other purpose than to tell it. And to tell her story.

But even if I'd known more, even if I'd given you a hundred glimpses of her, two hundred, who's to say that I've grasped who she was, there might be one more glimpse that I didn't see and don't tell, the vital one, perhaps insignificant on its own but that when added to all the rest changes everything, and without it the other glimpses mean nothing at all.

I look at a stranger who has a disturbing resemblance to someone I might've known. I look at something that might have been.

Before you were born, says Dad.

I see that my mother, like Auntie, was young once and shining with hope. There are all those things that people say go with youth, the roundness and smoothness and pinkness, all that but more, much more, is the hope. It's as if

she's been cut out of cellophane, with a lamp behind her.
And I see with a cramp in my stomach that makes me dizzy,
how he loved that in her, that youthful hope, how he
scarcely could bear his brush to leave her face, how he lin-
gered on her translucent skin and nestled in the arch of her
lips and painted over and over again the corners of her eyes,
how he painted the contrivance of clothes quickly and
clumsily, the strokes almost at random, so he could return
to where he wanted to be, and breathe with her breath.

There's a red sticker on the frame: 'sold'.

Sometimes, says Dad, one misjudges the moment when a
painting is finished. Get the shop assistant to take you to
the toilet. Be gone a while.

In his hand is a tube of paint.

I can't hurry, I say from the cold toilet seat to the shop
assistant impatient at the door of the Ladies'.

There's a hard bit to come. And I'm frightened on my
own, I add, because she has the face of a kind person and
so she shuts out the hum of the shop and now there's only
the white gurgling of the cisterns and a creak in the pipes
and the crunch of grit on the tiles. I peep out and she's
picking her nose at the mirror.

Your hair needs fixing, I say as our eyes meet.

She says I shouldn't say such things to adults but her
hands worry their way to the roll of hair on top of her
head. Time slows to the drip of a tap. I rip many pieces of
toilet paper evenly along the perforations and pull the chain
over and over as if I'm trying to drown a horse.

Only the eyeballs, he says. I tucked in some blue. I wanted
her to glare.

I should've looked at him at that moment, I would've
seen more. Not his action of putting the brushes and tubes
back into his pockets or wherever he put them, not that. I

should've looked at his face. Instead I looked in the wrong direction, I looked at my mother, my origin, shining. If I'd looked at him instead, everything afterward may have been different.

You remember the way she used to sulk, he says.

I would've seen he'd created her in my mind, just as he'd created her in his own, just as he'd created me.

The shop assistant is beside us.

It's a beautiful portrait, she says. It sold immediately the exhibition was mounted. Did you know the model well?

She's looking at Dad, not the painting.

My paintings have been badly hung, he says.

She'd pulled back her hair sternly while waiting for me in the Ladies'.

We did our best, she says.

I came to inspect, says Dad. And I'm appalled. An artist of my reputation.

It is your only sale, she says.

That makes my point, says Dad.

I'll never grow up, I promise in the lift.

His lips stretch hungrily, not a smile, it's hunger, like Auntie's hunger, but for something different.

I'll always be your little girl, I add.

As we walk past the glittering shops, I train myself to look only at his feet.

We drink coffee in a brown shop noisy with the making of espresso.

I drank this sort of coffee in many places, says Dad.

Sixteen teaspoons at her wake, all with pictures. A tower a pine tree two torches three castles a moon two stars a queen with a piercing nose a mouse two lakes a football and a hand. And afterwards we had only a moon and a hand to wash up when the two guests had left.

But then everything changed, says Dad. He's too angry to wipe the milk froth from his lips.

Yes? I ask. I'm pressing against the hard shiny laminex table. What happened?

The coffee bellows in the expresso pipes. Dad licks his lips, the machine subsides into gurgles.

What happened? I repeat.

The coffee trickles into cups.

As he goes to the counter for another coffee his trousers bag around his thighs sadly. I've left a coffee mark on the laminex.

I'm sorry, I say to no-one.

I nurse a brown paper bag of bananas on my lap as tall thin houses twirl by our tram. My hair snakes out behind me, its going back to the city. I'm timid about my first look at the sea. It might expect something of me.

I think I'll believe in God, Dad says into the wind.

He's tucked our tram tickets into his hat band where they ruffle.

Why? I ask but we're going over the last hill and the sea is vertical and shouting. Dad pulls the cord to stop the tram.

You didn't need to, says the conductor from the running-board. This is the end of the line. Trams don't swim. You from the bush?

I run down to the water and back to Dad, watching my footprints.

We take two bananas and leave the rest on the beach in the bag to hold down Dad's hat.

And to show us where we began, he says.

He's pushed up his trousers so they crush around his

knees. He carries my shoes and socks. Our pale toes grind the astonishing sand.

Because I'm not sure what I've done, he answers at last. He's throwing his banana skin to the seagulls. I do the same.

I have a dim sense of events, but not their intention or purpose, he says.

An upside-down sea snail sinks into its shell. I put it back on the rock which it will no longer grip.

Let alone their meaning, he says. It could be a problem in my work. There is a problem, I'm the first to admit. That's why I have the mirror in my studio. But a belief could be useful. In something other than art. If I believe in art.

Why does the mirror help? I ask.

But he's knee-deep in the sea.

This country doesn't notice its artists, he shouts above the breakers.

My best socks drip from his hands. There are stains on the bottoms of his trousers, like places on a map.

We are a whole white beach away from the bananas before he adds: If I understood events, it would help me about your mother. The guilt. The grief. The questions. Am I evil? All the time? Now and then? If I could feel, I'd know. I can't feel. And I want to feel.

He swings his arms around in giant Os.

I want to feel everything.

An O swings around to punch me in the stomach. I could crawl on my hands and knees in the drifting sand but a ribbon of light tumbles out of the sky.

I am here, I say to him.

His eyes adjust from infinity.

You? He laughs.

I twist, untwist my feet in the sand. The light bounces

away. He turns, walks back down the beach. I follow, kicking waves.

He's sitting on the sand. The bag and his hat are nowhere to be seen.

Those things don't matter, he says.

I wear wet socks on the tram. Seawater sloshes in my shoes. There are rims of sand on his trouser legs. This time my hair snakes back towards the sea. Our bodies are cold in the wind, but warm where they wrinkle together.

You and I, we can be silent together, he says.

She spoke too much, he adds.

Because there's no hat or hat brim, Dad shows me how to tear our tickets into long strips.

Not too narrow, says Dad. A steady hand.

This is a hotel bed one hot night when I went to the city with my father. See what I saw then—the lonely black hairs on his toes, the ripples on his toenails, his flesh slack around his neck, his singlet grubby along the hems as he choked on his snores through the hush of dawn. He was so grubbily mortal, my father, and that made his work more extraordinary than ever. Once.

We walk through the lunchtime crowds to Central station with our arms around each other so we don't get lost in any uncertainties.

There are many things a woman must and must not be, says Dad. It's important that you know.

On the train home, we suck gravy from square meat pies and burn our lips on milky coffee and avoid the stares of faces rocking importantly above briefcases.

She must never speak until the men in the room have had their say. Not even then, he adds. A woman must be an audience.

He opens a window to spit out a piece of gristle and let in the smuts. I see the startled eyes of a sheep against a paddock fence.

She must never compete, says Dad. A woman's mouth looks grotesque when she competes.

The train's stopped at a listening station, but Dad hasn't.

The lips twist in a most ugly fashion, he's roaring above his anger and the steam in his mouth. The carriage contemplates, hot with male smoke and throat clearing and the rustle of newspapers. Flaring with shame I hold the empty paper cut in front of my mouth and become preoccupied with crumbs, my lips could lose control at any moment and the men would turn to each other and nod and say: Yes, I see what he means. That child's lips twist in a most ugly fashion.

The man opposite turns a page of his newspaper and there's a photo of a woman tugging her jumper down tight and with those breasts it wouldn't matter whether she spoke or not, those breasts would dominate, would twist like corkscrews into thoughts, reason, governments, silence, papers hidden in briefcases, the words said and the words thought, twist and prise them apart.

I see what Dad means. Women are dangerous.

The driver must be off seeing a man about a dog, says the passenger with the newspaper. He looks to Dad for affirmation. Dad gives none. The train heaves a sigh and jolts off. The trees darken around a sign: Thirty miles to Griffiths Bros Teas. The mountains slump into night.

It may be that she feels competitive, after all, competition is an animal urge, says Dad, crumpling his paper cup and bag with the smears of gravy. But in that case she should stand at the back of a room. That way the man won't know. All he'll feel is her strength, strengthening him.

We're alone in the carriage. Dad notices the abandoned

newspaper with the photo of the woman, and hurls it out the window with his paper cup and bag. I hurl my cup as well. He puts my hand into the crook of his elbow. I drowse on his shoulder. Townships rock by like lit up birthday cakes.

A good woman is a helpmate and a friend, he says into my ear. And a companion.

I will be all these things, I promise.

We listen to our happiness.

Always, I add.

There are no taxis at the station. Only the wind tugging at the awnings of the butcher's shop, and rolling an echoing carton under the bus seat.

I brought a torch, says Dad, and we walk away from the street light into our own circle of light that moves and sways with our steps, sliding up tree trunks and over logs and past the desperate shape of a tree struck by lightning, and once pushing an owl back into the black hole of the night, but always sliding back, leaping away and falling back, like a wave on a white beach, like Dad's love.

Here I am, down here, my first painting, with my first easel. My father had taken me to a look-out to paint. But picnickers were there, sitting on a blanket, eating chicken.

A girl in a bright pink swimming costume shades her eyes. She's older than me but she thinks I'm already an artist.

These people are of no interest to us, says Dad.

My easel's stuck. I push and push. The girl comes closer.

You're supposed to be looking at the view, says Dad to me.

He tips his hat to it.

Absorb.

We absorb under the scorching sun. The shapes, which behind which and how and when. The light, foreground light, middle ground, background. The trees, the shapes they cut out of the mountains, the shapes they cut out of the sky. The whole and the details. The details and the whole.

I'm accidentally pressing on the mechanism on the easel. It gives way, the leg flies out. I nearly fall. The girl on the blanket laughs.

They've come to, she says.

I hide my bleeding hand.

I want you to paint exactly what I paint, says Dad. Always.

He's set up two easels. A new one for him. An old one for me.

He's pouring turps into the jam jar lids. I squash a mosquito against my legs.

A classic composition, says Dad. He's drawing shapes in the air above the canvas.

The horizon one-third of the way down, the river one-third across. The river turning back on itself three-quarters of the way down the diagonal.

The picnickers suck at their chicken. The sun sucks at our backs.

Don't overdraw, says Dad. The drawing comes in the painting.

I attempt five horizons, all wrong.

The trees, says Dad, and he hasn't really taken his brush off the canvas so that each line curls into another, the trees are to balance.

His brush wriggles into a stand of gum trees. I get my line indicating the river over as far as the corner.

Watch all the canvas, all the time, says Dad. Then stand back and look.

My white canvas laughs at me like teeth.

The girl in the pink swimming costume is breathing close. Her chewing gum moves in her mouth.

That's not what it looks like at all, she says to Dad. You've got the river in the wrong place.

She doesn't bother to comment on mine.

We're painting nature's beauty, says Dad to me. Not nature.

It's then I notice the turps rag sticking out of the turps bottle. Green shiny satin. A green shiny nightgown on a sunny morning.

The girl is joined by the other picnickers. Their thongs flap on the ground.

These are big mountains, big and strong, push them everywhere, make them big, says Dad, though his elbows are hindered by the crowd.

Trap those shadows, twist them over the plains, put in all the kinks by the river, all the black parts, see it, put it in, all the hidden parts, the secrets, the decay.

My mother's green shiny nightgown is a bottle stopper.

Anyone want the parson's nose? says one of the picnickers. It's a bit greasy.

Now the earth colours, Dad's saying. Broad strokes. Cover the space, fight back the shadows, lay in the warmth.

He looks across at me.

Stop lagging, he shouts.

I try another horizon and as they watch, a bright blue river.

The girl in the pink swimming costume stands in front of him. She puffs out her stomach.

Put me in your painting, she says.

Dad paints the river in silence, ripples that jostle and wrinkle and tug at reeds.

That bare space in the river, she says. You could fit me in there.

Dad's river is roaring through his painting, it whips light at the mountain, flickers down a cliff, hurls itself beyond the canvas. His face absorbed, still, he's inside the painting, in all that noisy violence. He doesn't look towards the palette, he feels towards its twists of colour like a blind man.

Usually you see faces that only exist when you're there, says Dad later. You don't imagine that when you go away, that face will sit down to dinner, ask people's opinions, fall in love. If you see that face again, you think it's popped into existence a second before you arrived. But that girl's face today was different. All her life stretched out before me. I smelled her parents between the sheets, I saw the length of her hair last month, I heard the air move as she died.

He's striding up the bush track to home.

For the artist, he turns to say, everything is for his use and power. Remember that.

He must feel like God, I call back.

Ants scurry by my feet, burdened, intent, mocking doubt. Nevertheless, I drop the turps rag behind a prickly bush.

He spoke in enigmas which I didn't understand then, and probably don't now. But I loved the riddle of them, since a riddle is a kind of mystery though less, because with enough luck or cleverness you'll put the pieces of a puzzle together, it's only a matter of patience, of waiting. A mystery is more, much more.

It wasn't just those enigmas that enchanted.

Nor was it just that orange pips, counterpanes, knives, nudes, wrinkles, sprouting potatoes, copper sticks, doilies, linseed oil, sudden pauses, garden paths, spectacles on noses, every miscellaneous thing was for his use and power,

and promised to come together and be reconciled in him,
he was the pattern that would subdue it all, that would
happen one day and I'd be there, not daring to breathe and
afterwards happy to die.

  It was that when he spoke these enigmas—pausing
before, his eyes just over my shoulder, his whole face
dropping down into his lips and pouching them forward
and his lips fighting the words back as if there was much
more in his mind to say but this was not the time, not yet,
the right time was to come—when he spoke these enigmas,
it was to me. I was his confidante. The pause, the lips
pouching, the pause after. He chose me to say them to. It
made up for a great deal. It made me believe we were going
together into the mystery.

Here, up here, I've painted the edges of the night. Of the
moon. The gum branch stinging on the wall. At our fence,
the edge of the twitching night.

Dad has gone again. To court, says Auntie, arriving again
in a taxi.

  I test my covers, tucked in firmly by Auntie. But my face,
it's uncovered, my ears, they're uncovered to hear a sound
more silent than terror. It was nothing. A bird peeping
again and again. Nothing. Only the wind straining and a
twig on the downpipe. An apricot dropping on the grass.
A lonely hen waiting for dawn. There it is, like a breath. A
pulse. She's in the air. Or in heaven, or in the ground,
rotting.

Auntie's hands shell peas into a colander but her eyes flick
around the voices on the radio. Good-o, she says and the
peas slide down the metal to jostle each other importantly.
I stand at the kitchen doorway, pick at a drop of uneven

paint on the woodwork. It doesn't come off. For weeks I've stood in doorways, in the bathroom, the hall, by his unused meal tray.

Auntie wraps pea pods in newspaper.

You know about Castro? she asks.

Yes, I say, unwilling to hear about Castro, waiting for Dad is enough.

She puts the newspaper in the kitchen bin, retrieves her hand quickly as the lid slams.

You know nothing, she says.

I imagine Auntie in Castro's country. She'd stand at the proper distance, head and breasts lowered, in the heat of the crowd as Castro drove up the winding hill to the shouting village, scattering irreverent hens that chose such a moment to chase worms. She'd run forward when permitted and reach out to finger the lines on his hand. While he'd stare at the road ahead of the jeep, not bothering to wipe the dust from his glasses. He'd only notice a mind that twisted into his, a face that looked away before he'd finished speaking, eyes that slid beyond his shoulder, shoulders half-turned against his approach, arms folded against his voice, lips that curled in an ugly fashion.

He wouldn't see her. He wouldn't have seen Mum. Only the green peas in the colander watch Auntie. Watched Mum.

It's easy at school because of Dad. He's the shadow behind the page before I turn it, the equal sign in arithmetic, the full stop at the end of every sentence falls at his feet. He's the calm voice behind the logic of geometry, the reason why the square on the hypotenuse equals the sum of the squares of the other two sides. He's Clancy of the Overflow, that crack rider triumphant on the distant ridge against the timid sky. He strides over the windy bones of the Australian desert, he stands on the fleshy pink map of the Empire with his hand in the heart of his coat. He roars cowardice out of his men as they sail to the world's edge. He's the boy under the apple tree knowing the still ground tugs at them both, he's the boy in the steamy kitchen watching the jubilant kettle, he walks alone out of the South Pole hut onto the splinters of ice, he laughs into the faces of patrons from his perch high in the Sistine Chapel, like Dante he glimpses the thirteen-year-old girl tossing her hair like a red flame in the gaunt streets of Florence and writes about heaven and hell for the rest of his life. He holds the bloodied knife in front of the echoing Forum.

At school they search my face for evil, I'm sure of it. The particular angles of my cheeks, the distances between eyes and lips, nose and chin, eyes and ears, the plane of the nose, look, look, that flaring of the nostrils, aren't those the proportions of evil?

But when I look up, the girls of the playground comb each other's hair, turn on bubblers, tie shoelaces. I look down to the lines of words in my books, I force myself not to look back till the end of the page though the sky drags at my face and the peppercorn trees strain at the asphalt. There's a flurry of giggling behind me and a footstep close but I get to the last word on the page, what I read I don't know but I gain the last word like a victory. Then look up. There are grey clouds over the peaked roof of the schoolhouse, there's a snake of water on the ground but the girls are still combing hair, turning on bubblers, tying shoelaces.

I need not turn the page. No-one notices. Or if I skip three, or go back to the beginning. Or where I'm up to, or what the book is. No-one notices. So I sit and stare at them, always an outsider. They shout and run, swallow each others' secrets, mince arm in arm past the boys. I stand on the edge of the asphalt. There are other strangers. A grand-mother in black calls to a new girl who runs into the toilets to hide but the old woman calls from outside the wire fence, the foreign words plead in the air long after she walks away, her legs so bandy I can see the length of the street between them.

I'm beyond the limits of their eyes, reciting spelling and times tables and dates of explorers. Sometimes when I must be amongst them, marching two by two up the stairs, I sing a list of conquerors. They swing round, lips slack in sur-prise. I'm invisible in the classroom, though I'd like to be asked population growths and yields per acre and could impress. I pretend to hear nothing, I'm a matt surface that reflects nothing.

In fact I observe, hear everything. But I don't have a friend. I'd have nothing to say to a friend. There is, after all, only Dad.

Dad comes back. And letters arrive.

Small minds full of hate, he says. Minds so small, it's a wonder they can lick a postage stamp.

He's taken the letter box off the fence down at the front gate to discourage the postman but it didn't work, the postman still leaves letters in piles on a flat stone where they stay, turning yellow more slowly than leaves, sodden by winter rains and crinkled by summer heat and silver snail slime stuck with dead leaves and twigs and dirt. We must not touch them, Auntie and I, we dare not, and over time the piles of letters topple off the stone and blow around the bushes. But the postman still delivers them, piling the latest lot nearby.

I'm doing what the law demands, no more, no less, he once shouted at me as I stood staring.

Spit flew from his lips and landed on the top envelope but it didn't matter.

He pointed to the stone, jabbing his finger to perforate the air.

This is where my job stops. Here.

I wanted to explain that these things don't matter but there are never words. So I stared at the way his spit magnified Mr, as if the writing on the envelope was shouting too, while he got back on his bike and pedalled off down the track with quick definite feet. And it came to me for the first time in my life that even if I had as much time as the piles of letters on the ground, it still might not be possible to convince some people that Dad knows what's important. But I know he does, and I'll be with him always.

Although he knows, he still wants to believe in God. I'm sitting in the little white wooden church on our road and he's leaning forward to believe, he's fingering the words on the fine paper of the hymn book, words about death and love, with the flat of his finger, not the tips as most people do, but so that as much of him as possible touches their meaning in the grey powdery air. The organist plays a broken chord so poignant that the grey powdery air shifts to prolong it.

In Dad's silence I'm left outside. I flip through the hymn book from beginning to end and all the way back but by the title page I know at last that I'm not necessary to him. He doesn't long to be with me although he killed with me. He sustains himself in his quiet man's world. He may not need me at all. In panic I reach out my hand and put it on his knee. I know the exact position of his body to mine, with my eyes closed in prayer I'd know, but I want to awaken in him a constant memory of me. He moves his leg under my hand's pressure, he sighs and stares at a watery stain on the edge of a crimson bible. The pew creaks under his change of weight. I take up no space in him. Only at the moment he invents me.

Amen, brother, shout the faces in the congregation, round, sure in the powdery air. They don't look at the words as they sing; their mouths are sharp circles, squares, circles in song as they look to the altar. They know that their Redeemer liveth.

Love, says Dad, isn't what's important.

Rain streams down his glasses but he doesn't unfold an umbrella, he never does, although he always takes it out with him, the mark, he says, of someone who knows the ceremonies. Even if it's hailing he doesn't unfold it, we take shelter under trees or on the porches of strangers' houses, leaving before they look out their windows.

Now he holds the umbrella out like a lance as if he's cutting through rain.

It's ridiculous, this notion that God bothers about love, he says. It's easy to get love. God wouldn't be bothered. That's not the problem.

I unstick my wet dress from between my legs, wipe the raindrop off the end of my nose. Nothing must obscure.

Then what is? I ask.

Splashing through chilly puddles behind his silent back, sometimes I wonder if we're both pretending he'll answer, if he needs my questions, if the questions are the ceremonies and the ceremonies are the answer.

Sometimes I think that if he loved me, he'd open the umbrella.

After he hits me he's always exhausted. I make a queenly decision to surrender as I see his hand coming down, as if

I had choice. I skid across the floor with no wish to apologise for the crashing easel, and now there's a wet painting on the floor that's surely a mirror image of itself. I always try to meet the blows face on, a hand across my eyes so he's a long way off down a tunnel of fingers. He sits down slumped on the sofa, I'm slumped against the wall. We stare at each other panting and hating. I know that love's not important. Acknowledgement is.

When sleep slips out from under their doors insinuating peace, I take Mum's dress from the wardrobe in my parents' bedroom. I leave the dry cleaning ticket on because it seems discourteous to remove although the staples prick through my nightgown, unwilling that the dress should be jostling again. I pull up the blinds while my chest thumps with the noise. White moonlight strokes the bed and the mirror and the gaunt wardrobe. At first my fingers are clumsy with the dread of staring into Auntie's cold eyes under the hard electric light, moonlight wouldn't suffice her outrage. I pin the bodice tight with clothes pegs. The seams that held out my mother's round breasts now slant in disappointment towards my armpits. I've tied up the skirt with string from the kitchen drawer and flounced some of the taffeta over it but the string flies apart. So I re-tie it, many bows this time, one on top of another, twisting the ears of the loops together and through each other and when I plump out the flounces again, the string holds.

Then I paint my face. Not with cosmetics. There aren't any now littering the dressing-table, and the bobby pins and spilt face powder and wedding photos and photos of me holding Mum's hand are gone and so are the dresses hanging in the wardrobe and the filmy blouses and the dressing gown heavy with comfort. Even the clinking hangers are gone. All that's left is the ball dress under the wardrobe, crushed against the board and old newspapers.

So I use Dad's paints.

I don't dance in the dress and the paint or walk through the house and moonlit room. I remember. That's all. Tonight, for example, I paint on a glimpse of her, we're sitting on the back steps and the hens are pecking on the concrete slab at the bottom just where the last step becomes the ground, it isn't sunny, it's grey, the grey of the backyard dirt and the scruffy lawn and the heavy air and the wearisome noise of the hens and their meticulous clawing and I say this to her and she laughs and starts to sing. She swings her legs out wide and puts her hands between them like a man does, easily, with nothing to hide, her legs wide and her hands folded into each other and her breasts and shoulders leaning forward, she's amused and easy with her song. It's not a song that leaves me out or includes me, it doesn't matter that I'm here. There are no mirrors, no poses. She isn't beautiful now, she isn't a woman or a mother, she's just a person singing and the song floats up past the clothes pegs on the washing line and up into the grey clouds. On my lips I paint her lips as she sings, on my eyes I paint her half-shut eyes. I don't do it sadly, or reverently, I'm not trying to be her, to bring her back. I just want to remember.

I do it night after night, waking up, expecting the floorboards to creak, realising that it's all over, all her sadness, going to their room, putting on her dress, painting my face and remembering. I know it's not important to her. It's important to me.

I watch myself in the moonlit mirror for a while, I remember, I watch myself remembering, I get sleepy, I watch myself getting sleepy, then I wipe off the paint with turps that stings, and the falling taffeta has the exhausted sound of dead leaves settling. I push the dress back under the wardrobe.

Auntie always waits outside the door while he hits me. I know she's there, I know it in the silence between blows, a silence so intense I hear the roof creak. She breathes, and sometimes she sniffs in the way she does when she's pushing her glasses up her nose, so I know she's thinking. But she doesn't come in. Perhaps she's counting. She rubs doorknobs until they're mirrors in case anyone wants to admire themselves in a doorknob, and arranges chairs so they dent the carpets in the usual places and when I cut bread on the cutting board in the kitchen she says make sure you're cutting with the grain of the wood not against it, and she insists I chew every mouthful fifty times. That's eighteen more than Mother. She doesn't say it's to flatten my stomach, her only pleasure in the future is that it's full of sorrow. When she went to the doctor in the next town, because the doctor in ours didn't have enough letters after his name, her dress dripped eagerly in the shower recess all night in readiness. She brought back cakes sticky with pink icing, one for her and one for me, so I knew I was required to listen to her.

She finishes chewing before she speaks, she always does.

The doctor, she says, was surprised at the depth of my suffering.

I lick my fingers. There's pink icing still caught under the fingernail.

He'd never seen anything like it, she says.

Like what? I ask.

Never ask a lady about her Insides, says Auntie. It isn't very nice.

My tongue swoops down of its own accord and extracts the pink icing.

But I'd accept getting written up in a medical journal, says Auntie. When I'm gone.

Would I get mentioned as part of your family? I ask.

You are only a moment in my life, she says.

And so, when he hits me and afterwards when he hates me, I haven't love, but I have acknowledgement and I float through the days on that, tied to it on a string like a balloon. Maybe tomorrow he'll talk. And so when I hear Auntie breathe outside and know she won't come in to rescue me, I scream loud and triumphant. Because I have hope, and she has none at all.

This is a yellow handkerchief in the breast pocket of the suit jacket thrown over the chair on the day Dad decided we'd move from the mountains to the city, to be near the galleries.

Not one gallery owner offered me a cup of tea, says Dad. I'd say my name and they'd look up catalogues.

He'd bought the handkerchief in some narrow city street, some shadowy shop full of tailor's dummies dangling tape measures. It shudders on the clumsy old-fashioned suit he's worn only to a wedding and a funeral, it's such a wintry fierce yellow the blue's shivering in it.

If I don't go back now I'll be forgotten completely. I'll give an exhibition and they'll say: Who's Geoffrey Montrose?, he says.

Auntie chews meat.

You could come and live with me in my house, she says. It's very central. A tram right at the door.

She's known why he went to the city, she wouldn't tell me, she's chased forlorn dust balls all week under the furniture while she refused to tell me. Now she wipes her mouth carefully with the serviette as if the food's stung.

Dad doesn't answer her.

You'll regret living alone, she says. The child will get in the way of your art.

Dad snorts as he cuts his chop.

I'll be on hand, she says after a while, more to her plate than to Dad.

When and if I'm needed.

She finds a crumb on her lips.

Of course, I'll be glad of a rest, she adds.

See how the handkerchief rushes out of Dad's pocket like fireworks.

Heaven help you two, says Auntie in the kitchen to me. How you'll manage, the two of you, I don't know.

Suddenly I'm pressed against her, along with a damp tea towel.

You'll come to me, won't you, when you need a bit of advice? she askes.

I try to manoeuvre the tea towel. She releases me.

Thank you, I say.

My arms are as straight as young plants, while it is she who leans against me, almost crumpling. Her fingers are bent like prayers or claws.

You've got a rough road ahead, she says. But I've made you a plan. Order is the answer to chaos. That's the rule I've lived by.

If you're living alone with your father, she says, you'd better know how to put a meal together.

We throw crackling egg shells into the kitchen bin. Egg yolks in a blue bowl rise pompously from their transparent beds.

*

And what about the undercurrents we drift in, you must do it too, not knowing you're drifting, you're just there, then someone, someone who's not drifting where you are, shouts: how lucky, how enticing, if only I ... and because of their shouts you notice you're drifting, but also because of their shouts you keep drifting, drifting and hoping, drifting and believing.

He's rented too small a house in my opinion, she says. You'll be living in each other's pockets.

She sniffs, pushes at her glass.

You won't be able to escape—careful, she cries.

Because the sun inside the bowl leaps high with my fork, whirling faster and noisier and may fling itself out of the bowl and splash light on the lino, on the picture of the silver knight riding on the fridge door his jaw arched with virtue, on the grimly shut canisters, on the stove that she scrubs as if no-one lives here, the sun may splash dribbles of light on Auntie.

She grabs the bowl out of my hands.

You're so careless, she cries.

We stare at each other, caught in the middle of another whirling, which I can't see though I feel the rush of air.

You have every advantage, she says. And what good does it do you?

At midday the smell of things mouldering into earth is strongest. Even stern gum trees melt amber and the yellow bottle brush no longer scalds. That's what I've painted here, my last walk in the bush before we left for the city. Always with feelings that words don't fit, other people find them, I hear them on buses, I reach and they're not there. I can be humbled by a cicada starting up in a tree. It knows its voice at least. Whereas I spent my whole life reaching, and only these daubs.

*

Auntie insists we take some furniture because the new house is unfurnished as far as Dad can remember.

But surely you noticed, says Auntie.

Dad drums his fingers on the shelf of his easel until she goes out of the room.

So we're in a van called City Movers with an outline of a grand and noisy city on the door. Gus, who'd introduced himself as City Movers at our front door so Auntie called him Mr Sitimoos till he explained, Gus stretches out his legs to embrace the spinning bitumen. His arms throb on the steering wheel. Eddie rolls cigarettes for Gus, he beds tobacco in the flapping paper, tucks in the errant brown curls, nudges the paper around the wad and rolls white trumpets for Gus' lips. Wrinkles rush away from his face. As we go past a township, shops on four corners can't reflect enough of City Movers' length.

She's a battleship, isn't she, says Gus proudly.

I wish Dad would nod with Eddie and me.

She's got ninety gee gees under her, says Gus. Do the right thing and she makes mince meat out of the hills. Eats them up. The other vans on the road, most of them couldn't pull the skin off a banana.

The van hisses to a stop at traffic lights. Two people watch from the kerb. I lean forward to be seen.

See how I got the jump on all these drivers? You got to know how to use space. I outmanoeuvred the lot. Done them like a dinner, says Gus.

It's a science, driving a van like this, says Eddie.

Between rolling cigarettes, he fingers a pimple.

That's the answer, says Dad.

What do you mean, that's the answer? Gus demands.

But Dad's voice has blown away in our slip-stream.

This boy hasn't got a clue, Gus continues, nodding at Eddie.

He doesn't know any answers. Only what I teach him.

Dad doesn't hear. I nudge him, while beyond the slants of Gus' forehead, valleys slide away.

I don't think it's the bloody answer, says Gus. Didn't you see how I pulled away from the lights? I'm up to speed already. Science is book stuff. You don't learn this sort of driving out of a book. This is an art. I'm teaching this boy an art.

But Dad stares at the yellow line vanishing underneath us. Gus snorts, balloons smoke. We pass a smell of barbecuing meat and the shouts of picnickers.

Nice to be some people, says Eddie.

Please stop here, says Dad.

Gus swings around to stare at me, Eddie, Dad.

Stop? he shouts. What do you think this is? A bus?

The vinyl seat sticks to my legs.

I'm the customer, says Dad, and I want to stop.

Ever since the traffic lights, says Gus, I've been building up a head of steam. Didn't you see how I pulled away from that lot? Smooth as butter. No way I'm stopping, no way.

Gum trees toss grey heads below us.

Gus only agreed to take you and your goods from A to B, says Eddie.

But B is where I say it is, says Dad. And it's here.

The van hisses into a clearing. My legs come off the seat with a thwack.

Put the furniture out here, says Dad.

Here it is, the edifice of our past on the escarpment edge, amongst the squashed paper cups and picnic servi-ettes, the rusting garbage bin on a stick, the screeching magpies. See the hubbub of shapes against the sky, a roll of carpet leaning on an empty bookshelf, my parents' bed upside-down, their mattress staggering, Mum's dressing-table cavernous and toothless where the drawers used to be, the sideboard doors swinging open like some awful invitation, books splattered against the undergrowth like dead birds. But the regency striped chairs that no-one ever sat in, they wait as they did in our hall, upright and forbidding. As if we could leave it behind, this city we'd built.

I'm the first to look back. I watch Gus' van blow a flurry of dust over it all.

Here are the huge lips smiling outside my window in the city . . .

lips stretched in such certainty that everything beyond the billboard is less real, the rows of houses and chimneys, the spikes of TV aerials, the office buildings, the traffic, the orange smudged sky.

The faces smile relentlessly.

What you want is a Coke, say the lips that know.

There's a man and a woman who have lost their fears, you can see that by their smiles, and the twinkles of frosting on the green glass Coke bottle promise to slake any thirst. They're so enticing, those beads, so eager to bring happiness, if only my arms were long enough I could reach across the traffic and trace my name, each letter dripping, I could etch my name in that promise of bliss.

Dad's footsteps echo through the empty house.

I'm starting again, he says. With my helpmate.

His hand on my shoulder is heavy with need.

Since we have no beds, we sleep the first night on the lawn in the front garden.

The grease from the fish and chips has come through the newspaper wrapping.

There are no mysteries after all, says Dad.

He throws the newspaper across the lawn, to land in dandelions. Now the fish and chips are swathed only in steam. I hold up a chip, blunt and glittering with salt. A man walks by with a dog on a leash and glances at us behind the picket fence.

Hello, I say, saluting with the chip. The man walks on.

Don't start unnecessary conversations, says Dad.

We suck white fish flesh from its whiter skeleton. Then we suck our fingers, as salty and greasy as the newspaper. Dad picks up the bones and sticks them upright into the earth in the outline of another fish.

I'll paint that, he says.

We wash our faces at the garden tap. I go back into the house and find our coats.

The sky is a canvas smoky with stars and pinned down on all sides by the lullaby of traffic. I slide on my coat lining until I'm not lying on buttons.

A belief in God, says Dad, offers few surprises.

He's making his coat into a pillow.

There is, after all, only art.

We lie without ceilings in this beginning under the smoky sky.

We're a long way from the mountains, says Dad.

His voice beside me is as companionable as the grass.

Did you ever feel that they were judging you? he asks.

I don't know what to answer. But the softness of grass cooling reassures, the night sparkles with newness, there seem to be no rules. I will ask my question.

Dad, I whisper. When's it going to happen? How long before we get there?

Where? he asks.

His eyelid trembles, his lips are still. I lie back after a while.

I didn't mean to be impatient, I whisper. I'm sorry.

The lawn is a ship and we sail on the rush of stars while the moon moves around the fish skeleton.

There's a face above me. A mouth so dark it may have no ending. But the body arcs down like a rainbow into sand-shoes.

I thought youse were corpses, says the man.

His shorts are wrinkled in a friendly way.

We live here now, I say.

We'll have two pints, says Dad from his coat pillow. And the same every day from now on, he adds.

His voice is as crisp as the air.

The milk in the cold bottles is blue with a yellow collar of cream. Dad twists the foil cap off with his blunt flat hand. I watch his adam's apple pump up and down. He wipes his mouth. There's a white streak of milk across his coat sleeve. He throws the empty bottle across the lawn. It skids against the dandelions and gleams with dawn between the fence palings.

He doesn't mention my impatience.

But the city prises out secrets, I see that morning. The slatted fences hide nothing, not even the frosty blades of grass behind them. The front doors crowd with the gossip of TV, the rattle of semi-trailers reaches down my throat, people at bus stops breathe white air into and out of each other. There's nowhere to hide, no deserted dirt road rimmed with scrub where I can kneel to watch sand drifting. I shelter in a shop doorway but a man blinks out through the pane at me. And on the running board of a tram, I hesitate.

Get inside, says Dad, and pushes me into the watching carriage.

He's about to put our tram tickets into his hat band.

No-one else does that.

Don't, I say. I'll hold them.

Warm bodies nudge on either side, insinuating that there'll be a disclosure at any moment. And there's no relief when I look up. The advertisements' gossip: Which twin has the Toni? Who's not using their Mum deodorant? Banish the pain you can't explain! Be regular with Ford pills. Are you too fat too fat too fat?

A woman opposite, her face triangular in a scarf, pulls a letter from her raffia shopping bag and a powder compact falls out open on her lap. She doesn't notice, she's reading the letter, and the compact is chipped with use and the puff grimy with caked powder and the mirror anxiously finger-printed because beauty is supposed to be all that a woman needs and this woman doesn't have what she needs, every-one in the carriage can see those anxious fingerprints and the twitching of her lips in the steamy tram and in the mirror, the twitching of despair. She folds up the letter, at last she'll notice the open compact and hide it but no, she's opening the letter again, and she sighs, and in the mirror are the decayed teeth of her despair, and now she folds up the letter and at last sees the compact. She snatches it away into the darkness of her bag, stands, pulls the cord and turns her back on the faces of the tram.

You must make a special note of today's date, says Dad. For when you write my biography.

Is that what I'm going to do? I ask.

She's nervous at the door of the tram, reckless through the traffic.

You can write: The great period of my father's work began on this day, he says.

I'm glad when the shadows of the buildings swallow her.

*

This is the house where I lived alone with Dad. Here is the door where I went in and out to school . . .

and I leave the key for Doreen who Does for us, who I've never seen and Dad hasn't either since on her Days he escapes and sits in the State Art Gallery so sullenly that people think he's the guard and ask directions to the toilet.

There's no mirror in his painting room, the closed-in porch. One day when he'd over-painted, too much fussing so I was exhausted with looking, he threw a can of linseed oil at it. The mirror was limpid water, a hundred gentle parabolas. When a piece struck my leg, it was green in its thickness and brown behind, a fraudulent thing that would've told Dad nothing.

You're my mirror now, he'd said.

You're in, shouts a boy in the street.

Shut the window, says Dad, while I watch the begrudging colour on the canvas, the begrudging start of our new life. I stand willing its triumph.

No I'm not, shouts a girl. You are.

This was our street scruffy with the shouts of play, tangled streamers amongst the parked cars. This is me at the window, my hand reaching for the catch to shut it . . .

to shut out the enticement in the street, the arm stretching, the bone turning in its socket, the arm still.

A girl is darting between the cars, plaits thumping, the boy laughing after her, and around a telegraph pole, her hair straining at the parting, a crack in a front tooth. He reaches for her, she holds down her skirt so it won't billow into his hand, his arm reaches out, she'll slip away but she stops, turns in his arms, looks up and down the street, raises her hands to his head, holds his head in her hands.

No-one's looking, she says.

He leans into her for a kiss, his hands uncertain at her waist, but her tongue is licking over the rim of his teeth and into his mouth's dark spaces, darting in and out, a cat lapping, sharp, quick, sure, red, and then they both lean into each other, settling, merging, and there are bumps along his cheek where her tongue rolls.

Shut the window and move, says Dad. You're standing in my light.

She leans away from him, finished, satisfied, but he isn't, he takes her face in his hands, he kisses her face, her tongue, teeth, wherever he can, her forehead, back to her teeth, tongue, I see his urgency, the way she pulls away taunting, the way his lips follow hers.

The floorboards creak, Dad's standing beside me, he looks out. I pull the window shut, I lower my eyes, I turn my back, but I can't shut out the enticement of the street.

I'd paint the stain on the ceiling, says Dad, if there were nothing else to paint. The intention doesn't matter and the meaning comes after. If I say the brush must go this way or that, I get lost, I panic, I overpaint, I do tricky things, then it's too late, there's layer after layer of mud, it's mud, I'm muddy, don't move.

He's painting me. There's an echoing sound to his voice. It reaches his own ears and falls away again and it's as if I'm in a room I don't share with him.

But if I paint from where it springs up in me, bright, wholesome, as clear as a shout, all I have to do is let the brush follow itself, and I and the painting are sharp, clean, good, he says.

I don't have a face, it's his, I don't have a body, it's his, I float, I don't breathe, I don't exist, I sink into the liquid which was my body, I'm free of me, as rounded as dreaming, drifting blue into the receding light.

And afterwards, he talks about the portrait.

There's a good strong shadow under its thigh. The knuckles on the hand are too pointed, that's how to tell a skillful portrait, by the hands, and those hands need more work. Its chin isn't clearly defined, do you see. And the eyes, the eyes are empty.

Every afternoon, in front of his work I promise to be nothing so it'll speak to me. I wait still abraded by the schoolyard faces, squinting so there's nothing beyond the painting or on either side, and I tell myself there are no black hairs sprouting between my legs or under my arms and no new breasts poking against my jumper like jeering fingers, and I wait. No thoughts about mother, and even the stone in my shoe doesn't exist. Dad doesn't exist. There's only his painting.

It isn't just paint. It isn't just a canvas.

And its edges slip by, I watch them go past, I'm being dragged to the centre of the painting, dragged, it's not my will it's the paint's, I'm there, reluctant to breathe, pulled at by light, shapeless with forgetting, somersaulting on colour. I'm there in the mystery at last, I must be, if only, if only, I've waited so long, this must be it, but I haven't changed, I'm still here, why haven't I changed, isn't this it?

But the painting won't let me ask that of it, it excludes me, it pushes me out, I'm pushed out past the colours, the shapes, the edges, I'm back on the floorboards and here's the ordinary sunlight. I'm pushed out but something inside me is quietened. And though the jagged day will shout tomorrow, it seems a long way off. And before it comes, something might change. Time might turn back on itself three-quarters of the way down the diagonal of the night sky, like the painting's composition does, or the schoolyard faces might lose their sharp outlines.

Who is the figure in the cart? I ask Dad.

He doesn't answer me.

I'm copying a painting of his, hoping. I only ever copy his paintings. I paint his mind, I paint his wishes, one stroke after another of his wishes so it seems to be my wish and perhaps it is.

If he allowed me to paint on my own, paint my own paintings, I couldn't even begin. We both know that.

Dad grunts under his breath, he throws back his head, his throat is long, he looks through the lower part of his glasses at his work. He steps away, steps back, dabs a leaf into life, darkens it.

I don't want to remember that you're here. Don't tread on that floorboard, says Dad.

In the painting, a figure rides towards me on a cart, a dark cart that draws all the road after it, while the bush strains on either side to follow, tree roots and sand and pebbles strain, the figure makes everything loosen its moorings, the figure is at the centre and all lines come together at the face in the centre of light, there must be a promise of more as the figure rides into my eyes.

I wait to ask again.

I lie my brush down, it rolls away from its resting place, I catch it before it drops to the floor.

Dad can't hear his voice, our city life chokes it, he can't hear it against these walls, inside this suburb, not now, but it'll return in its old resonance. We both wait for his voice.

You want too much closeness, he says as we walk at night. You invade. You cling. You cloy.

There are cracks in the footpath under a streetlamp. A long jagged crack in the cement between us. I stop but he walks on, slightly stooped, his hands plunged deep in his pockets, he'll reach to the bottom, bring everything out into the open.

You get in my way, he adds.

He turns around, the overhead fluorescent light casts such strange shadows that his face is a mask.

You're just like your mother.

My stomach scalds.

She mightn't have meant to get in your way, I say.

He snorts.

I follow him. Down suburban gardens there are lights at open windows and families framed like paintings.

All this damned need for closeness, he calls into the air. What's it all for? Tell me that.

I run after him.

It's an attempt to control, he says. An attempt to impose your will.

No, I say.

A TV flickers grey and white on a wall nearby. You're a dead man, pal, says an American voice. And he's going to die of laughter when he sees your corpse.

It's a battle of wills between us, Dad's saying. All the time you're at my elbow, preying on me, ingratiating, invading.

He comes towards me, my bowels quake, I think he's going to hit me, here in the street, in front of all these houses. But a dog barks at a gate, Dad turns, strides off, turns back and shouts: Walk on the other side of the street.

I start to run down the slant of a driveway but I must not run, not ingratiate, I slow down, dawdle across the street.

Our footsteps ring in the night. We walk together in time with each other. Perhaps that will anger him. I shuffle so now there are four heels, much louder than the rustle of hedges and the whine of TV sets across lawns. In every way, I'm determined to placate him.

Sometimes he was gentler in the mountains. When Mum was still with us, sometimes he'd come and find me, whatever I was doing in the house, he'd say: Let's walk and watch the light, and we'd walk out into the road hand in hand and with our free hands we'd feel the sun leave our fingers and fling itself off to the cliff face and along, all along the rims of the valleys, the rush of light in great gold jagged streaks and then the valleys silent, settling into night. In the sudden darkness when it had roared beyond the horizon we'd walk home, transparent. And Mum would be looking out the back window where there'd been no light, she'd be looking at the hen shed and the ragged lines of vegetables that were never very good to eat, it was the soil, she said, it wasn't the right sort and far too damp, she'd grown better when she was a girl living out west on the plains. When we'd find her standing there I'd imagine that all she was thinking about was the hens and the impoverished vegetables.

The footpaths slip behind me as we walk in the dark. I'm a traveller, strangely elated, because I'm stepping one foot after another into his wishes, but firmly. My feet move without my mind. My head floats above the hedges but beneath the stars. There are no streetlights here, only the sky hazed with neon. The street widens, stretches into blackness. I'm walking on grass, a park, I'm in a park and the ground catches itself up and flows into a hill. And at the top of the rise, a lamp-post, and on the glowing bench, he sits. I don't alter pace, I don't run to him, I keep moving closer like a memory. He's not watching but he knows I'm approaching, he rubs his chin uncertainly. He's right, in my need of him I have some power.

Now he puts his arm along the back of the chair to include the park in his lit body. I'm part of the park. But I come into the circle of light, and sit, the ground cold and hard under my bottom and strings of dried grass imprinting me with tangled patterns.

You'll get a chill down there, he says. Then I'll have to look after you.

The wind blows across the park and into his voice.

Come on. Sit up here.

The wind blows streaks of hair into my face, I come slowly to the bench, sit on the edge, lean into the dark, smell the damp earth, and by and by the dark silence rolls into me. Then, in case I think that he cares for me, he adds:

You want too much.

But I'm not going to stop wanting, I can't, that's why she had to die, and I know we're in a small circle of light that pulls the wind apart and rushes back into itself only when it's passed behind our heads.

I'm still waiting to ask about the figure in the cart. Because I've noticed as I've painted with him, stroke by stroke, his brush touching the colours on the palette, burnt umber, raw umber, lemon yellow, chrome yellow, ultramarine, titanium white he's using today, and my brush touching the same colour, or two colours, or three, his brush dipping in the linseed oil and swirling on the palette like a skirt in a dance, and my brush dipping and swirling, and his brush touching the canvas and coming gently away as if not to alert it, and my brush coming away gently, I've noticed that he doesn't paint the way I'd expect, but afterwards I say, ah, yes, of course he'd do it like that, as if there's part of my mind that's worked it out but won't tell, so I can't anticipate but only follow. There's a pattern to the way he paints because there's a pattern to the way he is, that's the riddle and all

I need is patience to understand the landscape of his mind.

I'd come home from school and Dad was in the closed-in porch where he now paints and he was vulnerable in his clumsy, heavy suit.

None of the galleries would have me, he says. After all.

He takes off his glasses and the rims of his eyelids are white, drained, but his eyes catch at, grip me.

They wouldn't so much as unwrap them, he says.

Paintings in brown paper perch on the sofa like visitors, timid.

Move them, he says. I want to sit down.

I put my suitcase down, I pick them up quickly, I must do it one by one, my left arm cradling, my right hand stacking, fingers making rips in the paper in my haste to take them out of his sight, to hide his pain from him. I carry them close to my body, my arms reddening with the weight, I take them to my bedroom where perhaps he'll forget them after a while. I rest them softly against the wall.

Make me a cup of tea, he shouts.

I see how carefully he cut the brown paper this morning, how precisely he'd stuck down the tape to impress. So I warm the teapot just as he likes, no shortcuts, I cradle it to test its warmth, burning my hands, and the tea-leaves, two and a quarter spoons, measured exactly, and I'm not precipitous with the kettle, I wait till it gurgles. And I see the blunt hairs on the back of his neck as I go back into the room, my mother would have shaved them for him, but all I can do is put her doily with the cross stitches under his cup. The steam unfurls. The grandfather clock ticks.

Drink it, I say.

If there's a great work in me, a truly great work, it'd come out now, he says. Now, in the prime of my life. If it's going to come out at all.

He raises his head.

I'd be better off without you, he says.

When he hits me the glassed-in porch is an amber box tumbling with scalding tea and the echoing sound of flesh on flesh.

But the next day, two bikes lean heavily against the wall, one large, one small, with handlebars like wild animal horns, but the smaller one has a white wire basket that could take a picnic with sandwiches and cakes and books and a checked tablecloth to lay out on the grass of a park. Dad opens the door quickly, he's shy at my excitement, his lower lip trembles in his generosity.

We'll go for rides together, he says. He pushes a pedal so it whirrs.

You'd like that, wouldn't you? he pleads.

I don't know how to ride it, I say.

I'll teach you, he says.

He stands at the central post of the rotary washing line in the back yard. He holds the post with one hand, the other hand is on my handlebars, and I ride round and round, a circle under the octagonal of wires, until there are tracks of broken grass, and I'm pegged to the pedals by his laughter, that rings so high it may topple over into a scream, and sometimes I laugh too, but always my laughter slides under his, so that he pauses, anxious, as the noise bounces off the orderly fences up and down the street and the solid quiet houses, and returns to him like a question. I take my time to learn to ride while he spins round and round. Tomorrow when he's forgotten me, this image will comfort: Dad stretched out between the bike and the clothesline, exhausted with appeasement, like a crucifix.

*

I was bred to violence so I knew its glowing whisper—yes, you may look aghast, there's no denying it had taken my mother and then how could I ever love myself once I'd lost my origin, but that's the point, violence was a long indrawn breath behind the deepest things and with that breath there was death and with that breath there was life.

Here's a picket fence and eyes behind it. I'd done a smooth turn on my bike, leaning into the corner with perfect control in front of the nonchalance of those eyes, but my pedals reeled as helpless as a cry forced out in a crowded tram by sudden memory and everyone looking ...

and now I'm on all fours in the gravel.

The girl who kissed the boy, the boy who kissed the girl, and a friend on white raffia chairs on the verandah. I thread the bike chain through the spokes, my knuckles brown with grease, my legs purple with the fall. There's footsteps on the gravel, and breathing. I'm too busy to look up.

You've got muck all over your hands.

It's the pigtailed girl tightening her belt as she does at school, wanting everyone to notice. And even then I don't quite look up, but something in the afternoon light is pulling at us with a strange inevitability, pulling at everything, even the weeds trapped white-tipped in the concrete cracks. I'll look at her eventually but only in snatches, when she's touching her eyelashes to feel their length or repinning the clip in her hair.

What school do you go to? she asks.

I accept that I'm invisible to her.

Yours, I say.

She doesn't try to remember.

What's your name? she asks.

Frances, I tell her.

It's a boy's name, she says. She turns away.

And yours? I ask to keep her here.

Rosie, she says.

I can see she likes telling. Rosie is a name with a pink bedroom and frilly frocks and a mouth that lifts for kisses. I turn the bike onto its other side so I can face her but be busy.

I've seen you walking by, she says.

It's then I look up, surprised to be acknowledged, but she's twisting her leg around, sockless, suntanned, shiny, to see that she hasn't trodden in something.

You're always holding your father's hand, she says.

My mother died, I say.

She puts her foot down, adjusts the sandal strap.

How old are you? she asks.

Eleven.

I'm twelve. So's Edward and Russell.

I look toward the verandah as if I hadn't noticed. I'd like to sit in its shade on those white raffia chairs or perhaps lounge on the steps, swatting flies.

But she's going, little steps so her skirt sways in dismissal.

Can I use your tap? I call after her.

She doesn't turn around.

Use your own, she says.

Nevertheless I prop the bike against their fence. I know they're talking about me, Rosie and Edward and Russell, I hear my name and giggles. I bend over the bike, turning the pedals to test. Several turns and the chain chatters.

The tap's out the side, yells a voice from the verandah. Not hers. Edward's. Or Russell's. Probably the boy who kissed. I look over the fence, surprised.

I take my time to find it amongst the cool dark monstera

leaves like giant ears and the stone foundations bulging with the weight of the house. I'll hear their steps at any moment, perhaps they'll all come to lean against the house and dig their toes into the brown leaf mulch and stare at the wisteria frothing the fence with purple.

The tap is stiff. I'll go and ask for help, or soap. But no, I want them to believe I'm strong and self-sufficient, as strong as them, someone who could hold her own, leaning on their porch and talking about . . .

What will I talk about? Now that the water is streaking silver into the dirt, I must think fast. I must make easy, casual, clever comments that will make them put their hands intently into their pockets. Girls in milkbars smile over the pink streaked straws of their raspberry milkshakes and say how are you going and see you later alligator great weather for ducks hot enough for you, like the endless square dance of traffic, I tried saying them wrapped in a bath-towel and rubbing the steam off the mirror and Dad knocking on the door.

You've flooded the path, she says.

Her hands are on her hips. I'm in such a hurry to turn off the tap that I turn it on instead and spray us both.

Now you're standing in the mud, she says.

My feet are large and flat and my legs grow out of them twisted and pale. She has brown polished feet but I am almost reptilian, I see, and could soon have scales.

Use your sense, she's saying. Turn the tap back on and put your feet under it and wash it off. Without getting everyone wet.

There's something about the slant of my feet, I have big flat feet, I've got very long wide toes and the tap has stiffened up again and this time I don't spray myself, I drench her.

I'm running white-legged and barefooted across the

bristling lawn away from the apologies she was too wet to hear but it's I who am exposed in this carefully clothed garden with its swept path and neat edges, I run slack-faced past the eyes on the verandah and grab my bike and stop only when I'm past the line of pine trees and safe on our back step.

These days the canvases are often blank on their pale umber priming. Rectangles of air propping each other up. One day a face but in the space between the nose and the chin, no mouth. And then a painting done on top of the last so I can see the earlier one, a nose glaring through a street scene, arms glinting through a storm at sea, a bowl of fruit on top of a house. And isn't that house familiar, its roof like an open face? And then one day himself, naked, edging through a forest of broken trees.

I stop looking. The front gate is heavy on its hinges. The door handle exhausts me. I walk quickly through the closed-in porch, opaque with its own emptiness.

I stay long hours in my bedroom, turning pages of books.

I stand behind trees and watch Rosie. I watch the way she reads, rubbing the page down flat with a fingernail, making the lines of print obey her will. The way she sits astride a suitcase, her upturned mouth red around an apple, careful about the pleating of her skirt. The way she talks over the wire netting fence to Edward and Russell, buckling at the waist with laughter at their jokes and giggling as if she might break and trying to hold her mirth in with her hand but she can't, they're too funny, she's wantonly helpless before their wit.

I'm heavy with longing to be like her.

She's so visible, tightening her belt and folding her arms so the cloth of her blouse tightens across her breasts, she's always playing with her top button to accentuate the flow of her breasts and pulling at the clip in her hair because of the vigour of her curls. She'd twist into thoughts, reason, governments, my father would believe she'd prise them apart. That's why she can take Russell's head in her hands in the street and kiss him with only a cursory glance to see who's watching.

She's cheap, Auntie would say.

But on sports days, I leave my pile of school clothes near hers so at changing time I can be near her power in the smell of oranges and sweat and hot rubber sand-shoes. But her breasts lift themselves like her lips to be kissed and she walks around the room naked, lush, proud, with apricot thighs she's bared on beaches to tan, she says we're all girls here, as if girls are blind. Full of longing I scoop up my clothes and turn into a shadowy corner.

It's her visibility I long for: the crocodile of children walking through the gate, it's her the eye is drawn to. The children shouting in the sweet shop, it's her the shop keeper serves. She knows she's powerful, in the merest things, as she bends over to straighten a sock or plump out her uniform, she knows. And when she looks up through her eyelashes I see the sparkle of some wild and secret joy. I lean against the wall, rest the burden of my envy. Rosie doesn't wait for anything.

I tighten my belt, shorten my skirt, pin up my hair. I undo my top button although there's only a knob of a collar bone to see. I watch people's faces and when their heads are about to turn, I'm feeling the length of my eyelashes. I smile, all the time, at everyone, so much a tic starts. I stare long after they've stopped talking so their eyes will slide into mine. I buy pink fingernail polish and sit on my hands when I'm with Dad, to hide them. I spend my days contriving. If I part my hair just a little more to the right.

If I bare my legs on the back steps in the midday sun. If I file my nails into points. If I pluck my eyebrows into Vs.

It's one of those summer Sunday afternoons so long and humid only the guilty are awake. Dad stands at the back door. His armpits squelch in his nylon shirt.

It smells of death, he says.

There are beads of sweat around his nostrils.

What? I ask, but fear.

The street. The suburb.

He turns around, a sheen on his forehead.

My work. Me. You.

The primed canvases empty of paintings watch me. He laughs, without humour.

Perhaps it's just an animal expired in this heat.

We have dinner at different times. He stands at his easel at night, stroking his unshaven cheeks, as if he could find in their roughness the secret he's searching for. I stare at the wood grain in the table top as I eat. Afterwards I sit on my bed, hair damp at the scalp and neck. The hot wind drags at our lives, drags the tree tops round like clocks.

Rosie wouldn't paint one stroke behind him, always behind, moving her hand, arm, body like his, moving her mind like his, making the same marks, making his mark. She'd grab the brush, she'd swirl the brush wildly into colour like a skirt whirling around the head of the dancer, she'd feel her defiance strengthening her.

I imagine talking to Rosie.

I've come to apologise for hosing you, I'll say, And I'd like to talk to you. I'd like to be your friend.

I'll stand one foot on the path, one foot on the step,

encouraged by the white raffia unravelling under her. She'll squint into the light, her hand surprised and shading her eyes.

Or I'll lean on the verandah wall, gazing into the garden as if looking for something forgotten amongst the precise stonework.

I live alone with my father, I'll say. I have for years. So I'm not good at talking to people.

She'll lower her hand, look down to the quarry tiles in squares on the floor. Leaves will drift on the shorn grass.

Rest your legs, she'll say.

The chair will scrape, but her hand pushing it will be gentle.

I walk past the house again and again but she's not there. Again and again I walk round the block but it's merely to smell the petrol spills at the garage and watch at the ice-works the rattling slats of a wooden conveyor belt, the white blocks steaming in the light.

But this afternoon, brown with heat, she's there, alone, reading a book, her hair hanging over her face, absorbed. I walk to her gate, falter, walk past. The clouds are heavy, growling, it'll rain soon and jostle people on shining streets into an impromptu familiarity. Afterwards they'll separate, laughing, eyes cast down, remembering they have homes to go to, front doors to bolt, but only afterwards. Because of the clouds, I push the gate open.

She watches as I walk up the path. Lightning jags over the distant traffic. I'd forgotten how far the house was from the road. I'll call hello when I get to that bush with leaves limp as my tongue. To those drooping poppies.

What are you doing here? she shouts.

Too late I call hello.

She puts down her book.

It's the weirdo, she yells into the house. Lightning slits the sky and is gone, so I'm unsure.

This is private property, she shouts.

I reach for words, like feeling down into a purse, down, down, but everything is zippered up, and when I get the zips to work, the purse is filled with air and the top of my head gapes.

I am close enough to see the cover of her book. The title. True, I read. Confessions. Squeezed out of me by the traitorous clouds.

I wanted to say hello, I shout.

Her head is bent low, her lower eyelids droop to take in the sight of my red face struggling for sense against the bursting sky.

Edward and Russell are framed in the doorway, watching me. She looks back at them and her eyelids are tight and she and Edward and Russell are enclosed together and I am alone, open, under the intolerable rain which ricochets around me and shudders across the lawn.

Suddenly, I'm lying in her back shed, under Russell. The dust on the floor is so powdery I could reach out beyond his feet and draw in it and the shadows in the garden shed are as familiar as those between sentences and his grey school trousers smell of Vicks Vapour Rub.

Don't yell and we won't hurt you, he says.

Dad and I had walked arm in arm in the first light after a southerly storm, we walked for the length of a suspended afternoon and kicked stones along the footpath so that puddles became rainbows and when they were still we strode across them into each other's reflections.

If I hurt you, he'd said, jumping back from the cascade of a passing car and pulling me back with him, if I hurt you, you must understand. I have my own torments.

Edward watches me struggle.

Weirdo, he says to me.

Their eyes glint above me like broken glass, but I can hear their breathing, their bodies twitching. They must know they're vulnerable like me. Whatever they want of me will soon be over and afterwards we'll talk. They wouldn't kill me just because I'm weird. Although the blood's clamouring in my ears and I might drown. I must understand them, that's what's wanted. Dad's need to hold me as if they're him.

Now Edward is sitting on my face. Saying that if I don't keep still, he'll break my nose. And he'll fart. And Russell's trousers are oddly open and a pink intestine, raw and sad as a cut worm, hangs.

Edward jeers at Russell. Doesn't he know what to do?

And Russell says he's done it more times than Edward, who's done it nix, nix, but a drop of water blinks at the worm's end.

I hear Edward's watch ticking as he pins my arms down. The drop of water falls off the worm's end into the dust, magnifies the granules, sinks in.

Sissy, shouts Edward, looking at the water.

I couldn't help it, says Russell.

He's burying the moisture with his toe and the dust's eddying and Edward's ordering:

Yank her pants off.

I'm not going to pity them, they're nothing like Dad, they know nothing, they fart and dribble and are absurd, how dare they, who do they think they are, I bite, bruise, roll, yell, Chinese burn, twist an arm behind a back, two arms,

I know about violence, I pinch, I exult to hear the thump of bone on dust, I thrust back the door bolt and in a dazzle of sunshine and air, I'm free.

But they leap behind, lunge, pull down my pants and I'm hobbled.

I'm lying in dust.

Bolt the door properly this time, says Edward to Russell.

I'm biting and scratching and yelling and stirring up dust and Edward's yelling—

Keep a grip on her can't you—

and Russell's got my hands together behind my back but I kick dust and legs until they both sit on me.

Get the skirt right up, shouts Edward.

Stop telling me what to do, I know more about it than you, says Russell.

I flail my legs but the boys hold them down, my arms but the boys hold them down, I'm weighed down by their bodies, their violence, but more, I'm stretched out in terror under their conceit.

It's their conceit that I'm dying of, the way they end at the tips of their bodies, at the rounded points of the knee bones that stick out of their wrinkled trousers, at their ears that jut out of short haircuts, their hair is cut short the better to hear but they don't hear, they start and end with a recitation of themselves, they breathe in and out con-tained inside their clothes, they notice nothing except what may flatter or insult.

I don't exist for them, I don't breathe, I'm drowning.

I'm the length of the garden shed, as long and dark with no will even to scream into the chinks of light.

My mother reeling in her nightdress, exposed, falling, falling on the folds of her nightdress, that I buttoned up afterwards, so no-one would see.

And the figure in the cart riding into the centre of light,

I'll never find out who it is, now that death seeps into me, I know it by the absence of vibration.

There's a lessening of weight. I breathe, twitch muscles, wrench my head around.

Christ, says Russell into the silence so I know my screams are like the ones in nightmares that make no sound.

She's hairy. In Man Magazine girls aren't hairy.

Well, they've got pants on in Man Magazine so no-one can tell, says Edward. But you're supposed to have real life experience, aren't you? You have, haven't you?

Yeah, says Russell.

You're full of bull. You don't know what you're talking about, says Edward.

I do, says Russell.

So is it weird or not that she's hairy? demands Edward.

Yeah, says Russell. It's weird. She's not meant to be hairy.

You want to go in her first? says Edward.

Me? says Russell. Not me. She's weird. I wouldn't want to put my donger in a weirdo.

Dust over me, kicked over my face, stomach, thighs, into my eyeballs, hair and the place between my legs, they kick my face, skull, stomach, thighs and the place between my legs. But they are gone. Silence. Somewhere a slam of a door and the sun winking through the slats on the wall.

Their lawn again, but I'm limping this time with the flaring pain, over the spiked lawn and the fiercely cut edges, out the gate, down the street, past the far line of pine trees, and our gate clangs to shut out everything behind me and the garden path steams after the rain as if nothing could happen but sunshine, and the stone step is warm with puddles and here are our walls that promise that I'll never need go outside again, I only need walk this distance between the wire screen on the backdoor and the doorbell on the front door, between one wall and another, with the little white covered table and its vase of flowers always visible from the corner of my eye. And the light from my bedroom window moving only with the turning of the earth; and the stain on the ceiling that could be a shoe, an island, a goat, a bus, a kiss; and the kitchen gadgets laid out in what could be a moral order. Why should I be so foolhardy as to go outside my father's walls?

I clung to promises because I was so young. No, that's not true. I've spent my life clinging to them, to the promises of clouds, stones, kitchen gadgets, paint, the upward curve of lips, silence, certain motions of assurance, the way hands go into pockets, knot themselves behind backs. I was so desperate to make sense. To impose a pattern. In its own way, an act of violence. And in the tension between the pattern and the chaos, there's the energy of hope.

And here's Dad, sitting in warm shadows with his eyes closed. I'm limping past him to wash everything away in the bathroom and scrub the bath and even the soap. And afterwards I'll never leave him.

I forget the loose floorboard.

I've been watching the storm, he says, eyes still closed.

A response is required.

Will you paint it tomorrow? I ask as I edge towards the bathroom.

A man could go mad in a storm like that, he says. Trying to work out if it's outside him or inside.

It seems churlish to shut the bathroom door between us now he's talking. I hesitate on the tiles.

I might be afraid of what the paint says.

Then I know this is the moment to ask though there are runs of blood drying black on my legs and the pain's throbbing.

Dad, who was the figure in the cart?

What?

He's reluctant to stop listening to the storm he won't paint.

Your picture. The person in the cart coming up the country road. Who is it?

Oh. That.

He yawns, opens his eyes, but doesn't see me.

There's no answer. Its function was to make people ask: who is that figure in the cart, he says.

Dad and I never talk about my body and now we need to. But we pretend that from my head to my feet there's a space. I drift around the house some distance above the floor, like a ghost, like his portraits of me where I end at my neck. I hear girls at school say: My father thinks I'm built like a tank. He says I've got hollow legs, the way I eat. You're like the south end of a north bound camel, he says. And my Mum says I've got to eat porridge because it sticks to my ribs.

But my mother is gone, and Dad and I never mention my body. I can't even tell him I need a new singlet. I leave a note for Doreen who leaves a note for Dad who leaves a note and money for Doreen who leaves a note and a new singlet for me.

Early one morning the softness that's my insides is hard, crunching against the skin's shell. When I draw down the sheets I see appalling blood. I'm seeped in it. It's slithering out of me, unstoppable, anarchic, female. Something I'd heard whispered about, but I'd run from the locker room before the sounds became words. I pull up the sheets, roll away the darkness. Crouch over a book, my mind crouching too. All the way to the last word. Don't think, don't look. Go back to the beginning, this time, read everything, all the descriptions, all the dialogue. I see nothing know nothing acknowledge nothing. I'm part of him, I have to be. I cannot be as helpless as Auntie, as Mum.

The blood's still seeping out of me. And with it, my hope. I was not born for this, my head's shouting. I was born to draw out the mystery with my father in bright colours. To go where no-one else has gone. To search out the inevitable in myself. Not be be wounded, like this. Contaminated.

I keep reading. The sun moves at my window, I keep reading. I must continue to live in my head, five and a half feet above the dust balls, the grit, the blood. Above the spell of reality. I read to save my life.

But blood is seeping, slithering, draining. Onto a white bed sheet.

Dad, I say, looking at the carpet, his feet, the pattern of his feet on the carpet,

I must go to Auntie's.

Then I whisper, though there's only us.

It's my Insides.

I hear him take a breath, pause, swallow.

Ah, he says. Yes.

We stand at opposite ends of the room from each other. The traffic sighs in the street.

Slowly I raise my eyes. Up his body, slowly, to his face. There's no light on his face.

Dad, I say, will I, do I, does this make.

I stare into his unlit face. He looks away, unscrews the cap on a turps bottle, screws it up.

Damn bottle's been leaking, he says.

He unscrews the lid again, exchanges it for the lid of another bottle.

Have you packed? he says. I'll go up the street, find a taxi, get you to the station.

He puts down the bottle, eager.

Dad, I say, will it be different? When I come back? Will things change?

I don't know what you're talking about, he says at the door. But your Aunt will sort you out. She'll set you in order.

There's a plastic space rocket on Auntie's kitchen wall permanently promising a blast off. It holds pencils and biros in its little booster rockets and on its fuselage there's a detachable note pad ruled up with grocery items to tick off. It's labelled My Shopping Trip.

Auntie gets down the notepad and one of the biros. We don't look at each other. I look at the note pad. She looks at the end of the biro. She writes: The Mle Organ. The Fem. Insides.

She purses her lips, scratches at a spot of dirt on the laminex. There's no dirt there. Her handwriting is fine backhand, as if it's fighting a strong wind. She writes: The Curse.

Why mustn't men know? I ask.

I'm taller now than she is and untidy in her kitchen. I'd never noticed that she stooped. She hasn't boiled enough water for two cups of tea. We stand near her stove, to get some heat from the hot plates for our cold hands. She gives me a spoon for my sugar with a picture of a blue and winding river on the handle. Perth, it says.

Why mustn't men know? I repeat.

As flies to wanton boys are we to the gods, she says. They use us for their sport.

I stir my tea. Above the laminex the noise screeches. The sugar takes a long while to dissolve.

Who are the gods? I ask. She has the same habit of silence as Dad. Words locked away, and the key reluctant to turn.

Men, she says.

*

It happens to every woman but we pretend it happens to none. I'm to mark the days on a calendar, to hide the calendar in a drawer. Not a drawer in the lounge room, dining room, bathroom, kitchen. A very very private drawer. Even the calendar is an affront. When I'm in pain I must call it a headache, I'm sorry I have a headache I must say. I must not swim, run, hurry, walk barefoot, walk in high heels, sit on damp grass, stand for long times, drink cold liquids, drink hot liquids on the days of The Curse, but I must not explain to anyone. I may have the power to curdle milk, rust metal, dull mirrors, stop clocks, I may be untrammelled violence itself, so I must rise stealthily at dawn to wash the cloths and peg them out, as unassuming as white clouds.

That's why men mustn't know, says Auntie.

She's pulling her dressing gown tight across her flat chest. She ties the belt in several knots.

I don't suppose you've heard that the Talks have failed again. She pauses to glare.

What talks? I ask.

The Summit Talks, she says. She's cut the bread so thin, the toast buckles under marmalade.

The West is incapable of understanding Khrushchev. He's a genius, that's his problem.

A piece of toast flies across the table propelled by her resentful knife. Now there's a butter stain on the cloth so carefully ironed the creases feel obliged to stand upright.

Why don't they understand? I ask. I can see the bundle of her knitting beyond the kitchen door, jabbed by its own needles.

Who? she asks. She's looking round, finding what I'm looking at, suspicious.

The West. Why don't they understand Khrushchev?

We. We. We're the West, she says.

You're the West and you understand him, I say.

I'm not the West, she says. The East is Khrushchev and the West is, well, it's no use naming names to you, you wouldn't know, the West is a lot of famous men.

She laughs.

Who cares what I think? Who am I?

No-one's meant to join in her laughter.

She's out in the garden again, digging holes, shaking the grey tentacles of presumptuous weeds. I'm not allowed to help because of my Condition. I turn on the TV to see grey children from America wearing mouse ears. Girls my age sing above breasts big as clenched fists. I unroll a bundle of knitting. It stretches across the armchair, down to the carpet, across the floor, down the hall. I wrap it up, put it back.

A moment later she's in the room. She hasn't stopped to wipe her boots.

Your father, she says, has he talked about your mother?

There's nowhere to hide from her eyes. And my own, ridiculously, are full of tears, as if I've always been crying.

No, I whisper.

But she's looking beyond my shoulder.

I've had a long time to think, she says. At the time, it was so confusing. But all these years. Not a word from him. I thought when you two came to the city, I'd be appreciated. But he hasn't been a good brother to me.

I remember what it was like to be my mother's daughter. There were circles, twenty circles, all over a page. I drew twenty faces, and afterwards a corpse like a cage with the animal gone.

They let him off, she's saying. That court did. As if he'd done nothing wrong.

She's agitated, pushing against me, the chair behind is

pressing into my legs. She's saying something important. Something outside those magic circles.

And I don't think they should've. He was, after all, guilty. All that stuff about him being the inheritor and maker of a firmament of greatness.

What stuff? I ask. When?

It was in the newspaper, she says. At the time of the trial.

People know Dad's the inheritor and maker of a firmament of greatness? My proud mouth can hardly make the shapes of the words.

That's what they said, she says. And let him off.

Let him off what? I ask.

She's harsh with scorn. You know what I'm talking about, she says.

Let him off what? I whisper.

You know your father killed your mother.

She's speaking as if those ancient circles had no significance.

He didn't do it alone, I whisper.

Of course he did it alone, she says.

I don't think so, I say.

What, do you think he called in the army? she asks.

I struggle amongst her polished furniture.

I'm sure he didn't do it alone, I say. And that other person, the one who helped him, they're guilty too.

What are you trying to say? she's shouting. Of course he did it alone. What would you know about it? You know nothing. You were only a child. You still are. I should be given some credence. At least by a child.

I don't contradict her any more. We pant in her room, her knitting on the chair, my body with the bleeding I must hide.

Your father and I were close as children, she says. You wouldn't know about closeness.

I do, I say.

But her face is cavernous with memories.

He'd say things, she's saying, that were either meaning-less or full of meaning. It was hard to tell. Nowadays I think he didn't know what he was talking about. But when I was a girl, I loved what he said. It was as if I'd stubbed my toe. I'd remember my feelings. Or find out I had them. He'd rush into a room and make me go out and look, say, at the wind, or at the blue of a gas flame, or the rainbow on a cicada and suddenly I wasn't alone any more, I was inside him, it was like seeing through his eyes and his eyes were much larger than mine. And then he'd forget, you know, it was as if it hadn't hap-pened between us, worse than if it hadn't happened, because I'd had something I hadn't known about, just for a second and then it was gone, irretrievable, he wouldn't speak for days, I was a stranger, he didn't need me any more, he didn't need an audience any more, I suppose that was it, and afterwards things would be greyer and drabber than ever.

He picks you up and at his height there's a fairytale, a view that goes on forever and then he drops you and you can't see it any more. He picks you up, and dumps you. And I've been dumped a long time now.

A blow fly drones in the silence.

That's what happened to your mother, she says. I see it now. I didn't then.

What do you see now? I ask.

Your mother got tired of being dumped, she says. She wanted to go off and remember who she was. Like I've been trying to do.

She sniffs. And wipes her hand across her mouth, a gesture she used years ago, as if her own spittle hurt.

But she didn't, I say. Go.

There's a soft buzzing from the carpet.

You're too young to understand, she says.

She knew she had to stay with Dad, I say. Whatever was wrong. Since he's the maker and inheritor of a firmament of greatness.

I wave my hands in the immensity of possibilities.

Love isn't that important, she says.

I know, I say. I'm not talking about love.

We glare at each other. I put my foot out, to hasten the death of the fly.

Was my mother close to my father, too? I ask.

She turns up the volume on the radio.

I'm standing, suitcase in hand, in the cold shining kitchen. She's wiping down the working boards, lifting her canisters, wiping away our conversations before I'm out of the house. She's too busy to let me put my lips against the bones of her cheek. I must wait, must watch her hands, grey with resentment. I look at my hands. Make them reach out to stop hers. But she doesn't see, she's ripping off the top pages on the note pad from the plastic space rocket. I read The Curse as she throws them into the bin.

Goodbye, I say.

She pauses in her wiping, jabs a grey finger at the wall above the sputnik.

There's God, she says.

She jabs her finger in the middle of the sputnik.

The angels are here, she says.

She points to the nose cone.

Men are here, she says.

She runs her finger down the fuselage, down past the tail fins, down past the red and yellow blast off flames, down to the point on the wall below the rocket.

And here are women. Me, your mother, you. That's how your father sees us. The ground to blast off from.

She runs her finger up the fuselage again, up to the nose cone.

Whereas your mother, she wanted to ...

Auntie pushes her hand up the wall as far as she can reach, fanning her fingers.

I make a choice, right there, looking at her fingers.

My father needs to be understood, I say. Because he knows about things. He knows.

My lips on her thin hair are stiff with certainty. When she holds the door open, I know she'll slam it behind me. Even her breath is cold on my face.

Don't say I didn't warn you, she says.

And if you look at the picture as a whole, ladies and gentlemen, you'll see that it depicts someone who stands in doorways. After childhood I didn't paint, how could I, when he scarcely touched the canvases himself. Sometimes in front of those bare canvases, I'd feel a rush of longing, the brush would glide so smoothly on the oils I knew, but didn't dare. He needed understanding. It was enough that I was near him. It had to be. Or else my mother would have died for nothing.

Self Portrait Two

Oil on concrete

3 ft x 2 ft, 3 ft x 2 ft 6 in, 2 ft x 2 ft

Oil on slate tiles

10 ft x 12 ft

Oil on venetian blinds

5 ft x 7 ft, 5 ft x 7 ft

You can put it off for years, the need to speak, to paint, whispering to yourself: my time will come. No-one expects it of you, it's enough that you hang the tea towels out to dry, we live this dreadful lie, pretending all that concerns us is that the tea towels dry thoroughly in the sun. We postpone that other voice, the voice from inside that orders: now.

There's certainly life in outer space this man was saying as I walked by. I'll tell you about this painting because it was such an extraordinary day.

For a start, there was a moon, I've painted it here, a white tunnel into the blue haze, and a bitter wind but the sort that's edged with joy, whirling around me and tearing off across the road and up the playing field past the school children in gym tunics, and my skirt whipped against my legs and strained to follow. Without that moon I would've kept walking on my side of the road, the side where scrub bites the tar, where people walk who don't want to be noticed.

And there was his shape too, an out-thrust bearded chin and protruding buttocks. With the green park noisy behind him and the sun and moon whirling in the wind, he made the shape of a Z. As if it was significant, that Z, as if everyone *should notice. And his hair pulled across a bare high forehead like a curtain, clearly he was a ridiculous man.*

There must be life in space, he repeated because the children weren't listening, they were scratching themselves and tying shoelaces and squinting into the sun.

It's a mathematical improbability that there isn't.

And put a whistle to his lips.

I was standing amongst the sand and ant hills and the egg and bacon bushes. He must've felt the pull of my stare. He looked across at me. And a girl who was just then unbending from tying her shoelaces, she looked too. In the uncurling of her body I knew there'd be trouble, the way her legs were brown and sure all the way from her white sand-shoes up to her gym bloomers. I knew I should pull my sun-hat down and walk deeper into the scrub.

She nudged the girl beside her and the three of them stared at the young woman with the floppy sun-hat and the dress with its hem let down again and again until it and the wearer were too old to get any longer.

The ridiculous man didn't take the whistle away from his lips. It stuck out from his face and the ball rattled inside, recording his breathing.

And one of the girls opened her mouth, there are many open mouths in my paintings, that terrifying moment before the words are hurled out.

It's the murderer's daughter.

The words rip across the road, across the green park. The man turns and walks into the noise. And I walk far away where words can't reach because only heat and the prickling of insects matter. Amongst the small bushes that whirr against my legs, the earth has the roundness of the globe and the sand is too hard for footprints.

A painter, you're thinking, but she has a great preoccupation with mouths, with words.

Paint often seems gentle, cruelty's only discovered later when the spell's gone.
But words, ah, words, they disgorge death now.

We've returned to the mountains but the people in the village don't speak to us. No-one remembers, at least not when I'm passing by. Only the butcher, eager with a rival down the other end of town and his sign: Meat You Can Eat.

Dad on his midday walks notices trees, twigs, weeds, ants laying eggs. Not the heads averted over rose bushes at front gates, dusters shaken out of front windows as he passes. These are not the subject of his paintings. But the swollen ant fingering the air as if birth is a thoughtful process, the ant makes him vulnerable. Once a pebble was thrown.

So smooth, he'd said. It must have been in the river in some form since the beginning.

What's the shape painted on the tiles? you ask. Why, it's only a pebble.

I'm Dad's housekeeper. I hang bright washing on the line and the clothes wrap around me wetly. I hold open the back screen door for the grocery deliveries. I time it to shut before the flies come in, droning heat. I look at the parting in the grocer's hair as he goes down the steps and I see it's crooked. I stand with Dad at his studio windows. His sighs streak the last light. Our lives are held at the end of the day inside the picture frames he makes. By the hope that tomorrow he'll be able to paint like he did when he was my age. My purpose is the rooms of my father's house. If a shadow passes the open door, it's only a bird.

*

Every week I walk to the butcher's. The butcher has a face as red as steak. The women at the counter move silently away as I approach, although on the sawdust my shoes make no noise. It seems too lowly in front of them to order sausages. The butcher always smiling helps me with the pronunciation of wiener schnitzel. I wonder how to cook it but don't ask.

Anything else, sweetheart? asks the butcher.

We're going steady, he tells the women, bobbing his head at me.

I have to repeat nothing else several times before anyone can hear. Tonight they'll be important telling their husbands what a murderer eats.

The butcher doesn't wipe the blood off his hands before he wraps up my steak in newspaper. The package has red fingerprints.

That looks ghastly, says a woman. They all laugh.

There's a leaf clinging to the back of my shoe. I want to tread it off with the other shoe, but don't. And on the other side of the butcher's window, between the strung up carcasses and two cardboard cut-out hens, is the teacher. I look away, look back but he's there signalling me.

Have I got a rival? asks the butcher.

Yes, I say. No.

I'm dizzy with moving back towards infinity where our eyes met under the tunneling moon.

I feel the whiteness of many round and watchful faces as I step onto the footpath.

I saw you in there, he says.

It's only later that I realise how often he uses unnecessary words, but kind.

And I wanted to apologise for my students, he says. Not that they're mine, he adds. Or that I could control them if they were. Or that I'd be sure I should. The right of the individual, you know, that's what's most important.

He's been holding his hands together as if it's a recitation.

I'm sorry, he finishes, and drops his hands so they swing at his sides like oars.

Things come at one so quickly, he says. And recede.

I swing my hands too. Yes, I say. I want to pretend I haven't noticed his embarrassment. In the mirror of the butcher's window, two people stand face to face swinging their arms.

I come from down the valley, he says. I'm just in the mountains as a relief teacher. So I didn't know, ah, the state of play.

I search for words to make me alone again. As I walk home through the scrub I'll relish this man, his white skin punctured by the hairs of his beard, his eyes floundering on the footpath then remembering to rise to mine.

Thank you, I say.

But he doesn't leave.

Thank you, I repeat. He stands between me and home. I can't dodge him, I won't turn my back on the direction I want to go.

The meat's dripping, he says.

It's true. There are arcs of blood on the pavement. They criss-cross each other. They criss-cross each other on his shoes.

The stain will come off, he says.

But I'm not sure. Because of the stains on his shoes, I let him drive me home.

I say he can't drive me the whole way, I don't want Dad to see, though I don't say that.

He has a small green car full of objects. He moves some off the front seat and puts them on top of others in the back, where they topple.

That's enough, that's fine, I say.

Although I'm sitting on a hammer.

The meat's still dripping but he's left a yellow plastic bucket on the floor so I put that between my feet, and wait for the church to come into view. We can't talk because of the noisy ricocheting of the objects in the back. There seem to be many milk bottles.

Here, I say when we get to the church.

He stops.

There? he asks.

We both look at the church speculatively. Doing this with our eyes, it's easy to say farewell.

The yellow plastic bucket is lying in the road. My skirt must've swished it out. I hold up the bucket like a flag. He backs in a cloud of dust.

I'd like to see you again, he says.

I wipe my mouth clean.

That'd be too difficult, I say.

Why? he asks.

One of us has to admit that we're incompetent. Besides, I'm anxious to be on my own to begin remembering.

I don't know how to tell my father, I say.

I hand the bucket through the window.

I'll write, he calls.

I laugh into the trunk of a gum tree. But turn and wave the meat, spreading more arcs. And worry all week that he might ask someone my address, and visit.

In my father's house, the house of my early childhood, he lives upstairs, I live downstairs. Upstairs is his studio, huge windows on the cliffs, watching the mountains, the sky, the bush. Downstairs is the main kitchen, the main bathroom, the laundry, the hall, the room that's always been my bedroom, the room that used to be my parents' bedroom. There's a door on the stairs. He walks past the door on his midday walks. He never comes through it. I walk in his studio, down the stairs, through the hall, the main kitchen, the main bathroom, the laundry, my bedroom. I never go through the door that used to be my parents' bedroom. There are enough whispers in the rest of the house, in the grain of dark-stained wood and just above the eye's reach, that flurry in the corner of the eye when the head turns.

For a long time after our return I don't open cupboard doors, wardrobe doors, drawers. It's a house of cupboards but I open none. I hang clothes over chairs, pile plates, cutlery, saucepans on working boards. I float on surfaces.

At dusk I stand at his windows with him near enough to feel the heat of his body. Outside it's blue, the bush, the mountains, the tiny trees below in the valley, all so blue that for the first few nights I dream we live by the sea. And we stand above it all, Dad and I, like sentinels.

Often I time my trips to the butcher's so I walk back through the dusk. If I dawdle, I turn the corner into our road and my lower part of the house is lost in the black silence of the bush. But Dad has switched on the lights of his studio and his windows on the cliff are blazing rectangles suspended amongst the first evening stars.

And yet, since I've met the ridiculous man, I've become a thief. Every day now it snows, soft and absurd, fastidiously furring the spiky blades of lawn, the stones on the front path, the pegs on the washing line, every tree trunk and tree root and leaf and branch and even the cliff edge until they become toys. And every day I steal from Dad.

I steal the scrapings from his palette. He tells me to put them in the garbage tin but I don't, I put them in a piece of paper and take them downstairs.

He doesn't want them, I say, I'm only taking what he doesn't want.

But I'm taking jewels from the altar, these flames, the cadmium yellow and cerulean blue and alizarin crimson and viridian green and vermilion, they swirl together in my shadowy room. When he crunches out on the white toy road I run downstairs, I gloat in my guilt as he walks in the snow.

I try to assuage my guilt.

Use more green, I urge at his elbow. The painting needs more green.

But I hold my breath when the brush seldom dips in the twist of green. When I set the table for lunch, there are just a few indentations. More when I clear away dinner, but not many. Tonight I'll hold an emerald in my hands.

When he begins a painting, stops, takes it off the easel, leans it against the wall, and the palette is almost untouched, my voice asks: Couldn't you use the colours again tomorrow?

I won't paint for a while, he says. It's a noise in my silence.

His hands have aged before him. They're still blunt, but the knuckles are spiked with bones, like claws. His hands are relieved to fall back, to be buried again in silence.

After he's gone to bed in his studio and I've closed the stairs door, I examine my hoard. As I gloat, he's above me, he's always above me, whether he's crunching on snow on the road or thumping the floor with his stick as he walks through the night. But with these jewels I'm hard-edged, a visible shape amongst the shadows, with colours in my hands, colours in my eyes.

When we stand at the window watching the snow drizzle into a damp evening, I avert my face. It may be he'll turn suddenly to ask for a bath to be run, a cup

of tea made, a sock darned, and see beside him the face
of a traitor.

Despite gossip, I always return to the butcher's.

I have something for you, says the butcher to me amongst
the stares. He smiles his sausage shaped smile around teeth
that could do good service on his chopping block.

He tips his head at the other women, back at me, back
at the other women.

No-one would want me to divulge a confidence, would
they?

Someone titters. They stand back, watching me.

Come on ladies, he says. First in first served.

Between his lips, words have a lascivious terror. He
knows about flesh, this man, about pleasing husbands that
might be husky.

We mustn't keep your families waiting, must we?

I'm held by his red face, his bustling black and white
apron, the jolly way he throws entrails into a bucket in a
triumph of blood, his pencil fast at the additions of legs of
lamb and corned hogget and half a pound of bones for the
dog. And a knife pins down to the counter a pile of misprinted pages from a woman's magazine. A man cradles a
woman's face in his hands. I want to be possessed, says the
woman.

Because of the colour misprinting, several women say it,
echoing. Possessed.

Now that there's only the marks of high heels on the
sawdust, the butcher turns to me.

Together at last, alone, he says.

He breathes out heavily, smiling, pretends he's worn
himself out for me.

You've stopped a young man in his tracks, he says.

My eyes struggle up to his in astonishment. Behind him

are displays of loin chops curled up like babies, all round his head, a halo.

I have?

His eyes evaluate the bone, gristle, fat of me.

A dark horse, aren't you, he says. After all.

He presses himself forward on the counter as if it was my body.

Naughty, naughty, he says. He's wagging a finger at me.

Didn't your mother ever tell you that you must be introduced properly?

He pounds another finger on the cash register. The tray jumps open.

An educated sort of bloke, he says. Like a walking encyclopaedia.

Under a pile of twenty dollar notes there's an envelope. He takes it out, turns it over.

Tim Birch, he reads. Name mean anything to you?

He keeps holding it, staring at it. There's a bit of pink sausage mince stuck on the corner. He flicks it off.

This woman here, see, she wants to be possessed. Possessed. As if it could change everything. Like an Old Testament prophet, dancing in the light of God, no longer drifting, dull, misprinted, but sharp edged, with eyes that split surfaces apart, like those windy days so searing that people and trees are bared into vulnerability.

Yes, I say. Because it must be the teacher.

He hands it across the counter.

Spent a lot of time on your behalf, he's saying as we stare at Tim Birch. Trying to figure out who on earth he meant.

I'm crumpling it with the heat of my hand, this passport.

Thank you, I say.

He leans on his crossed arms so the fatty flesh bulges.

You know, he says, the ladies all come and chat to me. Soul of discretion I am.

Yes, I say. The main street outside his window straggles under the sky. Only a few roofs offer diversion. I head for the door.

If you ah, he says, if he wants to keep sending you messages here, it's all right by me.

I hold the door.

I could slip them in with the sausages, he says. As a matter of fact, he adds, warming to the subject, you and I could have our own secret code. If there's a message from Mr Birch I could say: I've been saving a nice, juicy pig's trotter for you. Just so you'd know to look.

There's no need, I say.

I mean you wouldn't actually have to buy the pig's trotter and take it home and eat it, says the butcher. Not that there's anything wrong with them, lovely things, pigs' trotters, very underrated, a good pig's trotter is a meal in itself.

Really, I do appreciate your interest but there's no problem, I say.

I just thought of a pig's trotter because it's not the sort of thing you would forget easily, he continues. I mean if all the ladies were around and I said lamb chop it mightn't mean anything to you, but if I said pig's trotter you'd think, aha! a message!

Honestly, there's no need, Mr Birch, ah, Tim obviously couldn't remember my address, that's all, I say. Or my name.

The butcher leans across the counter.

I thought perhaps your father, you know, some fathers don't like their little girls having boyfriends, they—

He draws a line across his neck, chopping it off.

He sees me. His lips move back from their grimace.

Just a joke, he says.

Ah, I say.

I let the door clang behind me.

But he's rapping on the pane, pointing to the chops, the sausages, his mouth.

Reluctantly I swing the door open again.

Didn't you come for some meat? he says.

Tim Birch arrives at the church exactly at the time I suggest. I get to his car fractured by hurry and the fear that Dad may round the corner of the street at any moment.

No, no, Tim shouts through the passenger's window as I struggle with the door handle, but it comes off in my hands.

Allow me, he shouts, bounding out his own door.

He takes the handle, fixes it back on.

Certain theories suggest you may be arriving here before you left home, he's saying.

The handle won't stick.

Mathematically speaking, he says.

There's a man coming round the corner. But no, it can't be Dad, a dog's following him, and he's patting his thigh, encouraging the dog.

I don't have long, I begin to tell Tim.

I'll get you in in a jiffy, he says. He bounds back to his door. I watch both ends of the road. He leans across the seat, fiddles with the handle from the inside. The door explodes out.

Sorry, he says.

It's all right, I say, glad to be inside, though bruised.

We think you left home and got here. In that order. Home. Here. But why do we think that? Causality. And why do we trust causality?

Heaven knows, I say.

My skirt is caught in the door.

Don't worry, I say, but he's exploding the door again,

bounding out, lifting it back into place, helping it into its grooves. I wish I'd nominated a meeting place at the other end of town.

Why do we trust causality? he repeats.

When people don't exchange hellos, conversations become disorderly.

Experience, he says. We base our lives on that most suspect of things, experience. There must be some better way.

I don't have long, I remind him.

He pauses. Long? he repeats. I thought we were on a date. And you're in a hurry to go home?

Just to go somewhere, I say.

The location doesn't matter to me, he says. I wanted a talk. You answered my note. We got together. That's enough for me.

He sounds hurt, but starts the car at last. I huddle down in the seat, below the level of the passenger's window.

He notices this.

Is something wrong? he asks.

Not at all, I say.

Where to? he asks.

The bottles in the back crash. Though there are fewer this time, without being propped up by their fellows, they roll around faster. He must've tidied up his car for our meeting.

I don't know anywhere, I shout above the din.

I thought you'd lived in the district some time, he shouts.

I don't try to answer.

We pass the township. I see how rapidly the car covers the conversational ploys I know.

I'd been to the public library. It was poky, one room lined with the sort of stories shopping comes wrapped in.

The librarian was writing a letter. I could just read: Dear William, the rash has gone all pimply now.

She had eyebrows like question marks.

What are you looking for? she asked.

As usual, there were no words to explain.

An assistant librarian sat behind the catalogue making a chain out of paper-clips. She'd been at it for some time, it was already a yard long. As I came up she tidied it into a drawer.

I floundered through many headings. Bodies. Naked. Bones. Organs. Male, Female. Sex. I was there so long the assistant librarian eased open the drawer, slid out the paper-clip chain and continued working on it. Her purple fingernails were clicking behind me like beetles as I searched the shelf of Anatomy.

The Dictionary of Human Anatomy also expected its readers to know what they were looking for. At length I found a cross-section diagram of a man and a woman. The librarian heard my exclamation.

Success? she smiled.

Ah, I said, astonished at the male equipment for possession. I wondered if she and William would share my astonishment. I closed the book and declined to make out a borrower's card. Auntie had never got around to telling me about the Mle. Organ and the Fem. Insides. The Curse, had, to use the butcher's words, stopped her in her tracks.

I now steal tubes, paint tubes, my theft continues, it's cumulative, this betrayal, it has its own force, its own time.

They're in a kitchen drawer, these tubes flattened by his fingers, no-one can squeeze a tube like Dad can, pressing so hard the colour splutters, then dies.

I hide them because he'd misconstrue, suspect I have plans to paint the pictures he can't paint. But I have no plans to paint. That's not why I take them from the garbage bin, hide them here.

It's that these tubes, these colours were once much more, like a cloth that might've wiped a face, or a splinter from a cross. At the end of Dad's brush they whirled, whispered, cajoled, sabotaged, trumpeted. They slid in, slid out of the mystery that Dad knows, that I must find. They were part of it, anthropomorphising it, making it less, making it more. They were its familiars, whimsical, uncanny, alluring, forbidding, unbalancing.

But in the kitchen drawer, they lie in disappointment. And an empty tube of paint in the hand, that doesn't amount to an epiphany.

But love might.

I try many times to tell Dad. I sweep crumbs off the table-cloth slowly, I hesitate before turning on his studio lights at dusk, I look over my dessert spoon meaningfully, I cradle his turps jar in my hand before emptying it in the sink.

It should be so simple. Dad, I'm going to go out with. Dad, I met a. Dad, just by coincidence. Dad, it was bound to happen. Dad, it's about time I was allowed to.

I wonder how to answer the questions, how to explain the butcher, the windy day, the girl who shouted.

In the end I tell him I'm going to the township to buy light bulbs.

Dad isn't interested in light bulbs.

I'm making progress, he says at his easel. See? I'm getting back to my old form.

The canvas is full of straining. I shut the door quietly.

The woman in the corner shop is closing her doors as Tim parks the car. I have one foot on her doorstep. Her eyes squint in memory.

You? she says. We're shut.

But Tim's hands have made me persuasive.

Please, I say. I won't be able to see to cook the chops.

She grunts, lets me in. I follow her to the counter. Her feet trudge on the insides of her shoes.

Tim had touched my waist with outspread hands, he'd slipped them up over my ribs, up, up in an inevitability of delight, his palms scarcely touching me, so gentle there was air between his hands and me, up, up and then, as if my breasts hadn't been there before, as if there'd only been tatters of me, scattered, unknowing, he'd formed me.

I watch her use a long hook to get the light bulbs from a high shelf. I lean against the counter, something in my stomach squeezing when I think of his hands, his hands just there where my arm brushes against a jar of chocolate frogs.

A boy with hair in his eyes comes through from the back of the shop, throwing a yo-yo down, rolling it up, throwing it down, up, down, in slow motion as my stomach squeezes.

Go and run your bath, says the woman to him.

And her hands, putting the light bulbs into a brown paper bag, holding the bag by its corners, twisting it so it somersaults, falls, somersaults, falls, her hands are crumpled, smooth, crumpled, smooth. In her bed every night above the shop she must be sculpted by her husband, touched by the air under his hands till she becomes clear, like glass.

What are you staring at? the woman's voice is asking.

I find her eyes. They would look at her husband, those eyes, then half close, unguarded, turning into her skull in the astonishing pleasure.

Your hands, I say.

The boy is leaning against her hips, enjoying his disobedience, dropping the yo-yo in the space between their closeness and the counter. She pushes the light bulbs across to me, lifts a hand to ruffle his hair.

Do you paint too? she asks.

Oh, no.

I'm glad to lower my face to search in my purse.

I couldn't, I add. I just keep house for Dad.

She snorts at the mention of Dad. It was your mother I was thinking of, she says. The poor woman. I was remembering the way she loved to paint.

Everything around us is fierce with light.

Mum?

She was an artist, says the woman. You didn't know that, did you? You should.

My mother? I repeat. Are you sure?

He never told you, says the woman. Never told his own daughter. Well, I don't suppose he would.

Terrifying, the way words hurtle, wind is gentler and storms, sleet, snow, they come with warnings in the air, the sky, you can make ready for them more than likely, but words rip at your imaginings, while you whisper to yourself it doesn't matter, it doesn't matter, but you have two choices: that everything will be different from now on. Or that you didn't hear.

I'll ask Auntie about Mum, I tell myself.

To speak to Dad about Mum would be worse, far worse, than speaking to Dad about my body.

But I don't speak to Auntie, or visit her. I'm too busy. Busy waiting at the windows at the cliff's edge for Dad. Busy waiting for love from Tim, because love should mean everything to a woman. Busy stealing empty tubes of paint.

As if time will never end.

*

That's the glare of three chords from an electronic organ in a crematorium.

The glass doors glide, the minister walks in, he's leading a procession, no, he's alone on the thin carpet. Someone's economised on the making of his podium, it's barely bigger than his feet and his heel is cautious about the edge. He takes from his pocket the telephone message I left him, puts those few sentences that are Auntie's life down on the open bible.

Behind him is a wall of sheeting printed with a pattern of bricks but the shadows around the bricks are wrong, the light's streaming through the window from a different direction, past colonnades of rosebushes arranged for grandeur but shrunk in the rain.

We stand, Dad and I.

That's my Aunt digging in her pock-marked backyard, the way I remember her.

She must've struck a drain, the plumber who found her had said. Sometime earlier, she'd put all her belongings in labelled crates, with a plan to show where things were. The plan was the first thing the plumber noticed when he went in to complain on behalf of the neighbours. The first thing, of course, after the smell. The front door was unlocked. A house that small you were almost out the back door as soon as you walked in the front. She'd washed the last dress she'd worn, it was hanging in the shower bone dry, but that stiff, said the plumber, it could've stood up by itself.

The cupboards were stashed with food, he said, could've kept a family of ten eating for months, meat going off in the fridge, at least it was meat once. Miles and miles of knitting as if she hadn't known how to stop. The radio playing rock music full blast. Auntie bolt upright in a chair, a bit of torn out newspaper on her lap. Che Guevara dies like a rat, it said. But an old lady like that, said the plumber, she wouldn't have thought about politics.

Will she get written up in a medical journal? I'd asked the doctor.

Nothing unusual about the heart giving up, he'd said. Happens to every man and his dog.

When I was a child, her house had seemed bigger. Over the years, it had closed in on itself. Like Auntie.

The minister announces the hymn.

We'll only sing one verse, he says, glancing out the window at the rain on the roses and his car, and the deepening puddles.

What a friend we have in Jesus.

The organist forgets we're to sing only one verse. The start of verse two trails in the air.

My knees crack as I kneel. The minister's eyes aren't closed as he prays. Our eyes meet. For a terrible second, I think he's going to wink. The words have stopped. He's pressing a button on the podium. He presses again, again. The disturbance startles the bible. Auntie's life flutters in its pages.

I hadn't noticed the coffin. It must've been there all the time, discreet as Auntie would've wished, irrefutable however, the blank shine of wood. And the curtain rattling across on a rod to hide her burning, but for her there's no refuge, the curtain's stopping, jerking, rattling, stopping. The organist creaks in his chair. The minister steps down carefully from his podium, strides to the curtain, wrenches it but it won't be wrenched, he goes back to the podium, he's scurrying, not striding, he's pressing the button again, he bangs his fist on the button. There's a noise that could be a yawn, it's not the curtain moving it's the coffin, the three of us watch as it slides away into a black void, no it's not a void, it's a trapdoor, and behind is a chute and a furnace, and red flames around the coffin, red flames around Auntie, the big red clown mouth of death and Auntie plunging between those red clown lips. I'm on my feet knocking chairs over, as if now while she's in that clown's mouth I could reach her, touch her fingers, say the gentle words I could never manage to say, ask what I never asked, but the coffin's scarlet with heat, almost transparent, the timber's falling away, and at last the trapdoor slams shut and the organ bleats what a friend we have in Jesus.

The minister's handshake is as clammy as the air but I wait till his back's turned before I wipe my hand across my skirt.

The curtain of its own accord rattles across the final length of the rod and sways to a close.

In loving, I want to be possessed, I say to Tim.

His lips, so close to mine we breathe together, curve into the softness of his face.

Possessed, he repeats.

His skin whispers too in the sibilance of the word. His arm curving around me, his hand in my hand, they're trembling, I feel the movement through my body as if it's my trembling.

And who's to do this possessing? he asks.

We're sitting in the front seats of his green car, bucket seats that incline our bodies away from each other but we resist, leaning together in spite of the gear stick. Now at his question I ease myself back into the natural inclination.

Possession is a state of being, I say. I'm not interested in the details of how to get there.

He moves his legs between the accelerator and the brake.

But someone has to get you there, he says.

That's true, I say. Someone has to. I'd like it to be you.

He pulls me back to him, but I don't move my bottom, so only my head and shoulders rest against him.

Couldn't we, he asks, just make love? Like everyone else?

I lean forward, trace a circle in the mist on the wind-screen.

No, I say. There's no point in that. I want the extraordinary. An epiphany.

There's a silence. He's twitching behind me. His movements thicken the silence.

I love you, he says.

His voice is high pitched, pleading.

I turn the circle on the windscreen into a head.

I think, he adds, in his normal voice.

I make the head spiral over the windscreen.

But love, I say, isn't the point.

He considers this.

It's an achievement, he says. A milestone.

No amount of my wriggling makes his arm comfortable. I don't ask him to move because of what he's saying.

I may have been precipitous saying I love you but I want to do it, to love, he says.

I must lean forward. Bent over like that, I'm more intense.

I don't mind what you said. Love doesn't matter to me. It's possession I want. And afterwards,

My mouth so full of longing, like saliva, I can hardly speak: Afterwards, everything will be different.

Words were like this to me once: pools of white light where shapes might flicker if only I stared hard enough.

We're kissing, light kisses all over the face, kisses scarcely there, so quickly is each over and the next begun.

Here I've painted those kisses, remember them, when our faces were diaphanous with youth?

Tim, I say, reckless with kisses,
   Tim, what do you do about The Gap?
   He looks around at the battered seats and the car windows.
   What gap? he asks.
   Your arm is very uncomfortable, I say.
   We're separate, staring straight ahead at my picture of a head which is melting.
   When do you want this, this possession? he asks.
   He leans over to touch my knee and catches his cuff in the gear stick. I see his watch on his wrist.
   You must drive me home, I say. I'll be late putting on the potatoes. Dad will notice.

A few days before, I told Dad I was going for a long walk, and Tim drove me to his house in the valley. It was bright green, his house with the long rambling rooms, green, even the outhouses were green. The front door was red. Green paint splashed on the windows, red paint dripped on the steps. Kookaburra, it said on the gate, a name tied on with string. More like a parrot than a kookaburra, he'd said, throwing open the gate so far a hinge threatened, and the name plate jerked from side to side and his words were a rush of anxiety to please. He showed me to a large central room, high-ceilinged, spare, cold with a fireplace, a kitchen up one end, a table pushed against the wall, two chairs, a bed.
   The fire's gone out, he said.
   I looked through the paint-splashed windows. There was

an outside toilet with a sign, official blue lettering on a white background: post office. He blinked as if he hadn't noticed it before.

Humour should be allowed to be transient, he said.

We looked at it rebukingly.

A cup of tea would warm us up, he said.

It was the strained emptiness of the room. The table top gleaming, the draining boards bare, the stove gleaming, the bed made, no hair brushes, books, pencils, tubes, tins, bottles, nothing, no clutter.

Where do you live? I asked.

He was bent over the fire, flaying matches against the sides of a matchbox.

In this room, he said.

There were smear marks, I now saw, on the hurriedly cleaned table top and the stove, and bubbles of drying soap suds on the sink.

The room had four doors leading off, two on each side.

He looked up to see me opening doors.

Kookaburra has four wings, he joked on his knees, anxious.

There were more paint-splashed windows and clothes in a tumble on the floor amongst towels and tea towels and shoes and newspapers fanned out, recently hurled from perhaps the very place where I now stood. Every room was the same, light through dirty windows, and the tumble of his life on the floor. He watched as I opened one door after another, he twisted his head to see. I said nothing.

The kettle's boiling, he said as I closed the last door.

He couldn't find the teapot. I didn't help him look. I sat on my wooden chair in the big empty room.

The fire's not going yet, I said.

I can't do everything at once, he said.

He found the teapot shoved in a cupboard.

I don't know what it's doing in there, he said.

He couldn't find the tea. He opened cupboards, drawers, the fridge.

I make six pots of tea a day, he said. It must be close by.

It was there at last in a saucepan.

I'm hot now, after all that, he said. Are you?

No, I said, watching, still on my chair.

There were posters on the walls of other countries, places he'd never been to, places other people admired.

My life with Dad is so orderly, I said.

Hah! he said.

The walls of Dad's house are bare. His paintings partly finished and just begun rest against the wall face out when wet, turned into the wall when dry. He doesn't need to look at them, he says. He knows what they're like. They're already there all of them in his head.

Once I hung a painting, one that seemed finished, while he was out on his midday walk. He said nothing, I said nothing. He unbuttoned his overcoat, put it on its peg, called for his tea. When I brushed down the tablecloth after dinner, the painting was gone, down on the floor again, face to the wall. I said nothing, he said nothing. A week later, perhaps it was a year, he said that all his paintings were in the process of becoming, they had their own time inside him, that becoming was a process that had nothing to do with becoming something, things can just keep becoming and when they arrive, they stop, that's as final as death.

On my second visit to Kookaburra, I sit on one of Tim's chairs deciding not to make love to him.

What are you thinking? asks Tim.

He's pushing twigs into the flames. His jumper slides up

his back away from his trousers. The bared skin is palely freckled, vulnerable, so palely white that in the cold room it would mark, red.

This isn't the sort of room, I say, to have an epiphany in.

I stretch my fingers out in front of my face. The fingers are eager, reassuring, bigger than anything in view. They're bigger than the man on the other side of the room. He stands, walks towards me, towards my hands that could make a mark on him. He keeps coming towards me, pushes my hands aside, puts his arms around me, kneels so he's my height. I'm rigid on my chair, listening to his knees creak.

Do you think, he says into my hair, you could make do?

You'd like to know what it was like, wouldn't you, the details, this young woman naked for the first time with this man, the man lit by fire and joy, not at that moment ridiculous, without his clothes he wasn't ridiculous, he had one of those bodies clothes can't cover adroitly, she found him soft, pale, she lay on her side curving into his softness, turned on her back and felt the smooth curving heat of his skin, turned again and her hand was skidding across his shining stomach and over the hollows in the small of his back. She loved him for his arms almost boyishly thin, for the timid lines around his neck, the unexpected wiriness of his pubic hair, the way his eyes brushed over her nipples alerting them, the way he sculpted her again but this time deeply—

Well, why should I spend words or paint on something we've all done and must do again and again just to make sure we weren't dreaming? It's enough to say that whatever you make of these paintings, I too have had my moment of love.

*

Afterwards, I push open the door of my father's house and it swings as if nothing's changed. I turn on lights downstairs, throw down my bag, wipe off my lipstick so hard my lips burn, find the cold salted meat wrapped in a damp tea towel, remember tomatoes and lettuce, slice bread, set plates, cutlery on a tray, make another pot of tea.

Pots of tea herald events. Tim pulled on a singlet and insisted on making tea before he drove me home, his bare bottom goose-pimpling with the night air, the kettle sluggish on the stove. We kissed so long a skin of milk settled on the surface of my cup.

The stomach needs comfort at night, says Dad. Which cold food does not provide.

He cuts off meat fat with his penknife and pushes it over to the side of his plate. His movements are quick, deft, savage. I think of the way that Tim holds an ordinary knife away from the blade as if he didn't want to hold it at all. When Dad shreds lettuce, he pins it to the plate with his knife, and gouges out its crispness.

What are you staring at? he demands.

Nothing, I say. My knife gleams on the plate coldly.

This is Tim and I sitting under the space rocket in Auntie's kitchen. He was helping me clear Auntie's things out of her house.

Why don't you paint? says Tim to me. If that's what you want to do.

I trace the pattern of raffia weaving on the glossy laminex. One thread of fake straw under another, on top, under. I can almost see Tim's face reflected in it. Our faces in the fake raffia drowning, surfacing, drowning. And around the table, a metallic band.

I feel I have to wait for permission, I say.

We should've put saucers under our cups. Auntie would be grieved at such disregard.

Permission from him? asks Tim.

There's a ring of dribbles where his cup has been. He puts it down, it squelches into a new ring.

I suppose so, I say.

When I try to think about it, there's a metallic band around my head.

Your father will never give you permission, says Tim.

Do you think I've got rid of the smell? I ask.

Keep to the subject, says Tim.

Auntie pushing her spectacles up her nose towards her fore-head as she spoke, to seem more knowledgeable. Dumped. Her lips vibrating. Dumped. Her hand pushing as far as it could up the wall above the space rocket.

It'd take a peculiar bravery, I say, to act without Dad's permission. If I conjured up the bravery without him, from where I don't know, but if I did, there might be none of me left over for anything else.

When I'd left home to come to clear up Auntie's house, Dad hadn't waved goodbye. He'd gone inside. I'd turned back at the end of the street to wave, and the door was shut. Only sunlight slanting and bouncing back. So that when I paid my fare at the station, I kept searching through my bag as if I'd forgotten something.

And anyway, I say to Tim, without Dad I might have nothing to say.

Can I give you this permission? asks Tim. You know, if I encourage you. Buy paints and brushes. Keep you in supplies. Take your work around the galleries. I might even learn to stretch the canvases.

His arms rest kindly on the laminex. But I push the cups away.

You miss the point, I say.

I look out the kitchen door. Light doesn't move in the city. In the bush, it scuds across mountains, tree tops, pours into a valley, pauses a second and it's off again, spinning over the next mountain. Here, beyond Auntie's stretch of soil still in pot holes, the Sydney sun burns into the rows and rows of tiled roofs, paralysing them with the burnt out frenzy of rust. There's a confectionery factory with a clock tower. Say hello with a Chocko, it says around the face of time. Somewhere a dog barks tiredly on a chain. The chain rattles on cement.

Tim leans over, puts his arm on mine.

Is it because you're a woman?

How would I know? I say. I've never been anything else.

The dog stops barking. Tim's shoulders droop with thought. If I don't try to explain myself, he'll find a theory to prove that everything is explicable. When the need to understand is most urgent, explanations fail.

Rooms had this effect on me, they still do, certain of them, I don't know why, the fall of light, the direction of shadows, the time it takes to walk from one wall to another, the distance between me and the ceiling, I don't know, perhaps they are the shape of memories. In my Aunt's kitchen, with the glossy laminex glaring back at me, with Tim's heat almost my own, and that space rocket blasting off nearby, I saw. Not with my eyes, but the way the body sees in patterns and rhythms, inside the cells almost, as if that's where memory's stored. At that moment, I knew at last that he killed her. He killed her without any help, he didn't call in the army, he didn't do it with me, he did it alone. He killed my mother. I knew it in a flash of white knowledge. And then it was gone, I moved perhaps, sniffed, scratched, swallowed, belched and it had waned, I can only describe it like that, the ebbing, and where it'd been there was The Gap.

I find my handkerchief, wipe down the table top. It still glares back.

There's something I've got to find out before I paint, I say. It's difficult to explain.

I rest my head on my arms. There's only the whining of traffic.

Until I find it out, I'm counterfeit, I say. A counterfeit person.

Tim puts his arm across my shoulders. The firm, sure touch of an explanation.

It's freedom you need, he says. And there's one simple way to get it.

Tears fill his eyes from the perfection of the solution.

Marry me, he says.

I take down Auntie's space rocket.

Tim can create stillness by his touches, his touches between my legs become a succession of moments when everything goes so still I can see the spaces around things, before meaning crowds in and closes them together. The sort of stillness just as music finishes, when the stillness is part of the music, held, until it tumbles into the noise of meaning.

When a passing car lights his face momentarily, I believe he knows what I long for. We might reach out to it together. Then the car is just a speck in the distance.

But when I'm scrubbing floors or hanging out washing, when the distraction of touching has gone and I'm alone, I know that only Dad knows how to find what I long for. Only Dad.

It's just a matter of trying to paint by yourself, Tim said.

The salesman ripped off sheets of brown wrapping paper. Tim paid for the materials, peeling money out of his wallet and patting the change in his pocket with pride.

To please Tim, I painted a picture at Kookaburra. I battled against the oils. I over-painted, scraped off, over-painted, until there was nothing more the rectangle could hold.

Tim stared at what I'd painted.

Is it about us? he asked, his hand expectant at my waist.

In the end, I painted the scene from Dad's studio. For good measure, I included Dad. Contained within the window, which opened, so the eye could encompass him and slither out.

It'll probably be a masterpiece, said Tim.

I felt I'd never be able to introduce him to Dad.

But my brush could scarcely inch across the canvas. The painting was full of pre-conceived and consciously con-trolled lines, over-explicit in a wish to be something more, so that one almost pitied the artist. And it was filled with other people's lines, Modigliani, Munch, Matisse, Dad. Mainly Dad.

So now I peel carrots for Dad's soup, pushing the shav-ings with my knife over the edge of the wooden table and into the bin and the carrots glisten with relief. While I cut them, life is very simple. It used to be that way all the time, before I stole Dad's paints. Or so it seems now.

I was not meant to be an artist, I say. After all.

It's simple when I carry the meat home through the scrub. It's the pity in Dad's work that no-one will buy. The pity, for weaklings like Auntie, Mum and me, and the power. One day a critic will see. And I'll be there, at the back of the crowd. Which he will know, impatient in their applause.

I have this daydream often. It makes me devious. I time
its ending before I reach the studio windows. He's speaking into the microphone. My daughter gave me her life,
so I had the peace I needed, the understanding, he's saying
to the audience. Or on days when the gum leaves crush
voluptuously with summer perfume, he says: she is why
I paint.

In Tim's house, the painting I did rebukes me. It's there
when I lie in his bed, when I drink a cup of tea, huddle by
the fire, put flowers from his garden into jars. It rebukes
me with my temerity. In the end I take it home, and hide
it in the kitchen pantry. Dad hasn't gone into the pantry
for years.

We ought to marry, says Tim.
    We're at a look-out with a neat chart of rivers and pad-
docks below and dusty roads and clumps of trees. Even the
trees' shadows are circles.
    I turn my back on the view.
    He knows he has no grandeur. Only in his kindness. For
the rest of the time, he moves his arms too stiffly on the
sheets, too quickly, someone else's gesture in an armchair
in a smoky room, he borrowed the gesture, glued it on
himself, it doesn't quite stick. So many men are like this,
fiddling with the waist bands of their trousers in their kitch-
ens. Their wives, boiling potatoes for dinner, are pleased at
the familiarity, that's what men do, and the wives suck
potato from between their teeth during the thrusting in the
dark over the years, and later turn in their beds and listen
to the night.
    We are both, in our own ways, counterfeit.
    I'd like to get married, he says. It'd settle something in
me, not completely, but there'd be something certain,

something to hold onto. And it'd be good for you to get away from your father.

If you won't marry me, says Tim, there's no point. This affair has got to lead to something. Some resolution. One way or another.

I know Tim's face so well, the way it cuts into the sky. Despite his theories, nothing seems unexpected.

Don't you want it to go somewhere? he asks.

As if I have a collection of desires to be taken out, evaluated, ranked, and then swung back over my shoulder.

What about Dad? I ask. And Dad's house?

I think of Dad grunting, his brush lingering in the air, the daylight dying. Watching the trees scratch out the sky as I set the table. Coming home from his walks singing silly love songs and humming through the spaces of forgotten words.

He could have a housekeeper, says Tim.

Someone who'd wonder why the canvases are so often blank. Who'd turn on lights in places undisturbed for years.

They say in the township that he's well off. That he used to be famous, he says.

He takes a breath, stops. There's a space in the air.

After a while I ask:

And my mother? What do they say about my mother?

Nothing much. The talk's mainly about him. Oh, that her people disowned her when she married your father.

Why? I ask.

He had some sort of reputation.

What for? I ask.

I don't know. It was all a long time ago. People just remember—he waits for the scorn of kookaburras to subside—impressions.

Have you heard that my mother was an artist?

No, he says. What did your father think of her work?

I don't know, I say.

I walk along beside the wire fence that restrains the unwary. I feel into the space inside me, that history of me I can't touch.

Anyway, he says, following. The past has nothing to do with us. I don't mean you as an entity and me as an entity. I mean the two of us together. Us. The third that's formed with us together. The us. And these things about your parents, it was all a long time ago.

I can't be an Us with you, I say. I merge with my past. I am my past. All I can hope is that I'll merge with Dad.

I walk away from him, climb rocks, walk with scratched legs through scrub, climb a cliff, walk down a concrete path. He catches up.

I saw your tears just now. It must've been terrible, losing your mother like that.

I had to lose her! I shout.

I could spit his sympathy back into his mouth. And he sees it, sees my shrillness.

It's obvious that you're still grieving, he says. It explains everything. Makes everything add up.

There are tourists coming towards us, a man in a T-shirt bulging apologetically with fat, and a woman with a camera held against her eyes.

As clear as two and two making four, Tim's saying. Although, did you know, it's now thought that they don't. Add up to four, I mean. In our very act of observing them, they become something else. Like an Us. A new entity. Because we don't just observe, we participate.

What's that to do with us? I ask.

He drops to his knees.

You don't know anything, I say.

Please marry me, he says.

There he is, ridiculously on his knees amongst the twigs, unaware, buckled over, fumbling with both hands in his coat pocket, his body twisted. Under him, ferns smash. His glasses, heavy with concentration, slip down his nose. They leave behind pink half moons and palely crinkled eyelids. He's pulling out a small square box of pink satin, pink as the marks on his nose.

There's all the absurdity of a significant moment. The woman tourist smiles below her camera.

Still on his knees, he cannot pull hard enough at the catch on the pink satin box. His knuckles are purple with effort. I turn, run, I'm long legged in escape. Rounding a corner, I look over my shoulder. His elbows jerk out from his sides like hen's wings as the catch on the box slides suddenly into place.

I sit on cool grass, a pulse at my temple pounds in shrill hatred. He's nothing to me, a stranger, he doesn't know me, he touches me blindly, he only knows his need, he doesn't know mine, we are separate. I stroke the soft grass, it strokes me into an ecstasy of hate. I don't want to leave Dad, I can't, not yet, I must wait, there are things Dad and I have still to be to each other. I can't leave Dad's house. I'm hot with hate. Let him take his pink box with its diamond ring, make him throw it over the cliff, I will it, will it, now, now, lift up your arm and hurl it away. And throw away with it the trickery of touching, go back to the room you live in at Kookaburra, shut the door tight. Leave me alone with my father.

The woman comes down the path, the fat man following. Her camera swings from her finger. I stare at the grass.

Excuse me for interfering, she says.

I keep staring at the grass.

Excuse me.

The man clears his throat.

She pauses. Well, I just thought someone ought to say. Your young man back there is in a real state.

I don't look up. The man shifts uneasily on his sandals. We tried to help him.

Her husband nudges her on. There's a silence. We're jerked out of it by the raucous cries of birds soaring down the cliff face.

Don't you think you ought to go back to him? she says.

We all listen to the echoes.

When I feel the chill of the ground I go back to the look-out. Tim is bent over the fence, watching the distance, hair streaking his glasses in the wind. Pebbles crunch under my feet. His bottom stretches the material of his trousers. He straightens a little when he sees me, pushes back his hair. The wind blows at us from a long distance. I hear on it the miles of brown grass in the valley struggling to live in the sun. I stand beside him and look at nothing.

We'll go back, he says.

When Dad paints, I say, he keeps on long after the good light's gone, he can't tell that it has, he needs to be reminded. And he forgets to eat if I'm not there and wonders at the pains in his stomach. And he needs sometimes to talk over the day's work, I think he needs to make it real. And, I add—

I seem to be shouting, there's no need, I try to whisper but my voice still shouts—

The truth is, I can't leave his house.

Tim always lets me out at the church. There are wattle trees in the yard, jovial puffs of yellow against the white splintering paint and times of prayer group meetings and meetings of the Ladies' Auxiliary to discuss knitting bees and a note that the Rev. Smillin (Master of Divinity) because of other commitments will only lead the praise to God every fourth Sunday.

Can't you wait to marry me? I ask.

What for? he asks.

I don't know, I say.

Will you be able to leave him one day? he asks.

I don't know, I say.

Amongst the twigs and silence, he keeps his eyes on the steering wheel.

This is how it's to be resolved then, he says.

His shoulders are hunched.

Yes, I say. I open the door. I put my foot down on the dusty road. A white moon floats above us. It's not a tunnel in the sky, it's merely an object suspended in space.

Just a moment, he says, feeling in his pocket again, his body twisting again.

There's no point, I say.

He's handing me the little pink satin box, it's on the flat palm of his hand, skewed on its hinges.

A memento, he says. Put it in a drawer.

He flips the lid open, the box is a fish mouth, gaping, skewed, toothless.

There's no ring any more, he explains. I dropped it.

You dropped it? I repeat. Over the cliff?

Dropped, he says. Or threw. I don't know which. I don't remember well enough, I don't have enough information, if I knew all the quantities, measurements, dimensions, the masses, the velocities, all the variables including a more exact comprehension of neuromuscular controls, mind-set states and hand-eye co-ordination, then I could be more precise.

From now on, I say later to Dad, I'm giving up those long walks.

I'm washing out his brushes in turps. Violet carmine, azure, indigo, it all turns to grey in the wash jar.

I was beginning to think, says Dad at the window, that I'd be fending for myself soon.

No, I say. No danger of that.

I watch a swirl of Lamp Black fade into the grey. He seldom uses Lamp Black, seldom uses any of the colours he's used today.

This afternoon, for instance, he says.

I'm sorry I was late for your afternoon tea, I say. There'll be no more instances.

I'm waiting for him to stop talking, so I can stand beside him unafraid. Standing together at the window we are in some sense equals.

But he won't let me.

This afternoon, he persists, alone at the window, when I had to make my own tea, I found I'd run out of sugar up here.

It's the details that disturb.

Sugar? I repeat.

So I went downstairs, he says.

But you don't have sugar in your tea, I say.

The details that are part of a whole.

To the kitchen, he says.

The whole that's part of the details.

He's not looking at me, he's looking at the trees pulling the black sky to earth.

I do know my way to the kitchen, he says.

I'm leaning against the cold sink, with silver trickling over the bristles and the drain gurgling.

Your own house, he says, is like your head. If you must, you can remember everything in it.

His voice relentless. I've never noticed the clipped edges of the consonants, and the long vowels that push everything out of the way.

And find everything in it, he says.

I turn the water on faster, it swirls in spirals of silver down the drain, nothing can be heard above the rush of silver.

Did you find the sugar? I ask later when it's quiet.

I had to look everywhere, he says. Everywhere.

So he must have seen the painting.

I have two weeks of precise events. I cook elaborate meals, I stitch all buttons, even the ones that are holding, I make lists like Auntie's.

Dad often calls to me, he's now planning paintings in his head, he's painting them there, he's not bothering to lay out the paints on the palette. He talks about his paintings to me and I listen, my back to the tubes of colour with their lids screwed tightly on. I nod. I look at him. I don't look at the tubes. We both know I don't look at the tubes.

And the pink satin box, I hide it under the pile of clothes I've torn up for rags. But I keep thinking of Tim's hands.

One day crisp and yellow and blue with sun, I'm on my knees, my skirt tucked up into the legs of my pants, I'm scrubbing the pantry floor, I'm wondering whether to go to the extent of prising dirt out from between the floorboards, suddenly I'm using the bucket water to wash my legs down, I'm adjusting my skirt, I'm walking past Dad's windows, I'm walking through the scrub, I'm buying a stamped envelope at the post office, I'm writing a letter on the back of a shopping list someone's abandoned on the counter. The pen doesn't work and when it does there are blotches of ink in the crinkles of the paper. I'm starting at the top to leave room for all the words I'll need to use, I only use two lines.

Dear Tim,

I'll marry you.

*

Threatened with the loss of Dad, I become wiser. I see that when Dad stands at the window, it's a pane of glass restraining the wilderness. He could so easily be fragmented, he taunts it every evening. If only I'd known before.

I see when I hand him his hot water bottle that he shudders with the shock of heat. And when we chew our chops, he's uncertain, swallowing uneasily, fearful of gristle.

I'll manage, he'd said, as soon as I told him about Tim. He asked no questions about Tim. Not about how we met. Nor about our new life. Nor about how I felt.

I'll manage, he'd said.

I knew he'd shut the door firmly behind me. And when I looked back there'd be only the blankness of sunlight.

I knew when I'd visit, I'd see a man in the middle of empty canvases, in the middle of chaos. Who wouldn't start unnecessary conversations.

I won't come to the wedding, he says. I've got too much work.

But I get out his suit, I brush and iron it, air it, it hangs in his studio on a wire hanger, swaying with its own weight, he doesn't put it away, he dodges around it to stretch his canvases.

At least, I'll be able to say afterwards, at least he must've been thinking about coming.

He no longer asks my opinion about his work, he no longer tells me his plans. He stands in front of his canvases when I enter, he's secretive about their bareness, as if I've never known.

I'll hire you a housekeeper, I say.

I'll manage, he says.

Here I sit in Dad's studio, crocheting a button latch on my wedding dress.

*

I hear with relief the front door slam. Dad's tread on the stairs. He sees me, grunts to himself, I'm not usually in here except at his bidding.

The door blows open, the satin rustles. He looks down the stairs to the door, to the shaft of light.

I'll go down and close it in a minute, I say.

He hangs up his coat, puts the umbrella in its stand, picks paspalum seeds from his socks.

These are our last days together, I say.

But he doesn't speak, he stands in front of the easel. He's looking at his tubes of paint if he's seen, checking they haven't been unscrewed. He's never mentioned my painting in the kitchen.

We should talk, I say.

Lately he's taken to brushing down his easel with an old shaving brush, showing he can look after himself I suppose, though I've never thought of dusting his easel. He's fastidious about it, every protuberance.

There are things, I say, that we should talk about. That we haven't.

Swish, swish, goes the brush.

I don't put down my work, get up, close the door, put the kettle on as he wishes. I sit crotcheting with white shining cotton, and the slippery white dress moves in my lap.

The door will slam if you don't shut it, says Dad.

He's sitting at his easel, legs splayed, humming under his breath, waiting for me to do his bidding. I keep crocheting, watching the hook, telling myself I'll get up in five more stitches, ten, fifteen.

He doesn't hit me these days. He hasn't for some years. I don't remember when he stopped, it was gradual, a long slow forgetting, or perhaps it was that I changed, that when he turned around, there was no-one there.

I do one last stitch and prick my finger. Blood runs into the white shining thread, it's now brown in the tufts, the whole loop is brown.

Do I have to get my own food already? says Dad.

I put down my wedding dress, I go to the studio kitchen, fill the kettle, light the gas, empty the teapot, go down the stairs and shut the door, come back, lean on the working-board, look out the window. It's on the side of the house where Mum used to look out. I'm looking at the area that was once her vegetable garden. It overgrew with weeds quickly, the vegetable plot she used to worry over.

When I was a child I was scornful of trivia. And have been till now. And yet it's my life. These tiny unremembered acts that women have always done, that Mum and Auntie did, were experts in, they make me gentle. They make me conscious of my absurdity.

Dad, I realise in a rush of knowledge, isn't conscious of his absurdity. But that doesn't matter. It doesn't matter at all. He's conscious of more important things. Much more. Which I'm leaving behind.

I rouse myself, spread butter on bread, cut cheese. The kettle boils. I take the pot in, steaming, I put it down on its mat on the table. He's still on his stool in front of the easel.

When I'm half-finished my tea, he comes to the table and takes his, he crushes bread and cheese into his mouth until he can fit no more, he doubles up more in his fingers.

There are things we must acknowledge, I insist. That you must acknowledge.

I'm already flagging. I lean back in my chair. It takes energy, this insistence. He washes down the bread and cheese with tea, opens his mouth to the steam, pours tea into his saucer, waits for it to cool, pours it back into the cup, goes back to his easel.

I'm beginning to think I'll only be partly formed by the day of my wedding. Tim's fingers might never take me to that place beyond despair. They might become as emptied of hope as finished paint tubes. We might make love at night and afterwards lie listening only to the fridge switch on and off. But here in Dad's house, here where I most deeply love, this is where I might find it. If ever I were to paint, it would be here.

I go over to my dress, crumpled on the chair. It's a dismal thing, little more than a bag, I can't imagine my angular body making it splendid. It shines in its crumples with its blood-stained loop. I think of how Tim runs his finger down my face, his lips down the length of my body, my body waits, guessing where his lips will end. I'm touching the shining dress the way he touches me.

But you won't speak, I say to Dad.

I'm holding the dress and staring at him. He's staring at me, no, beyond.

I've constructed this device. First, this tab, you pull it, see, just here, you pull and there it is now, the old scene gone, and then this. Let it carry your imaginings to a place where you walk in wonder, there's no horizon, no sky, nothing to limit you, you thought you were bound and struggling on wet glass but now you're not, you're not concerned whether you walk, run, fly, you're lost in the place where there is no Gap. I couldn't paint anything for this part of the device, there is, I'm afraid, only this space.

I put down the dress, collect the tea things.

I won't go to the wedding either, I say.

But I do. I go. Dad goes. The three of us are there, Dad and Tim and me, and the minister's brought an old lady along, the cleaner, who's agreed to oblige with a signature. The minister's come especially to the church on our road, he's left his other commitments, turned the key in the rusty lock, opened the door into the brown shadows, turned on the lights.

I'd love to play the organ as well as sign, says the old lady. No charge. Do me good. I learned the piano as a girl, my mother wanted me to take my place at parties, parties were like that in those days. But I never did, I was too shy then.

She sighs. The minister inclines his head at the thought of shy parties. She sits at the pedal organ, up the back of the church, near Dad and me.

She's sprightly on the keys, sometimes too sprightly, remembering parties she could've played at and didn't, and the pedals lag behind, groaning with air. The church is as it was in my childhood, the air still powdery grey, the bibles worn at the edges. The paint spots on the floor are still there. And a blue carpet, I don't remember it, threadbare at the entrance under the insistent music but running up the nave with the wish to be grand and ignoring a hole here and a notch there. But when it meets another stretch of new blue carpet up in front of the altar under the feet of Tim and the minister, then it has its fulfilment, it is indeed grand, a full sweep of Prussian blue that on the fierce golden summons of the Wedding March sweeps from one open side door to another and out into the haze of forever.

I've never noticed before how enticing Prussian blue is.

Dad draws himself to attention, holds himself straight and erect. He's absurd, my father, he competes with the rituals, holding his breath and drawing in his kneecaps like a schoolboy.

When I'd brought Tim home, Dad eyed him above his tea

cup, refused to look away when Tim upset the cake stand. Tim had sat on a chair, the wrong chair, half-way down the studio and I didn't like to resettle Tim for fear of further accidents. I'd run between Dad's sofa and Tim's chair, unnecessarily passing teaspoons.

On occasions like this, Dad had said, there are things a father ought to know.

He had no trouble making his voice carry.

Tim, with a glob of chocolate icing on his chin, felt precipitated into shouting his qualifications as a husband; his job, his salary, his family, Kookaburra.

It was a hot afternoon. Tim kept easing the sweat in his collar, the dampness of his socks.

I'd watched Dad during Tim's recitation, seen Dad lift the little finger of his right hand away from the handle of his teacup in an upside down V as if he knew so much about tea-parties he could trust the air to balance his cup.

When Tim had gone, I'd fussed around the studio sweeping cake crumbs, hoping Dad would speak. He didn't.

I put my arm on Dad's arm. The organ roars. Dimly I realise it's not the Wedding March any more, it's Mademoiselle from Armentiers, we're at a dance in the community hall, I've walked by those dances at dusk and seen the eager polish on the floor, the men in shorts and long socks, the women whirling dresses and lifting their hair from the backs of hot necks. We're only at a dance, Dad and I, and then we'll go home, the house that's always been home, our real life will restart with a cup of tea.

Mademoiselle from Armentiers

She hasn't been kissed for forty years

The minister's frowning at the organist to stop but his arms are helpless in his surplice. He comes down to the first pew, he's going to run down the aisle past us and wrench the organist off her seat, no, he's going to leap-frog over the empty pews to her, no, he grips the back of the pew and chafes, hobbled by decorum.

Dad sees his agitation and pulls at me. He wants to begin my wedding. We begin walking the walking towards it, we're walking up the carpet inexorably, walking into my new life under the swirling sky of music.

But the minister's holding up his hand under the noise, a sign like a policeman's in heavy traffic. Tim looks around, and the minister's waving his hands across each other, Tim's waving his hands across each other, they mimic each other, gesticulating to us.

The organist hits the finale:

Inky pinky parlez vous

just as Dad's shouting into the silence, I think they're trying to tell us something.

You're on the wrong side, says the minister. Change sides. And something more appropriate from the organ please. We are, after all, consecrating a marriage.

Dad and I change places. Tim turns back to face the altar. The organ pauses and then swoops us defiantly down the carpet.

Love and marriage

Love and marriage

Go together like a horse and carriage

Dad's jacket wrinkles at the elbows in a whiff of mothballs.

And then in that whiff I realise at last that I'm leaving the hope that is in him. Loss streams before me up the ragged carpet. I drag at his arm as we wait for the minister's cue, and the music whirls around us in a dance. Dad looks straight ahead, the moment demands it, he's set his face against my departure. Only his adam's apple is vulnerable, it works up and down stretching the old skin on his thin neck that I should spend my life caring for. The neck of an aging man I see, the papery flesh of a prophet.

This I tell my mother

You can't have one

You can't have one

Word by word, inexorably away from Dad.

If you stayed with me, you could be my amanuensis, he says.

I clutch at his jacket, his lips surely did not move, no voice could rise against the jangle of music, it is impossible. I look down the stretch of blue. It was impossible. It was only my own bright longing for the glowing oil paints, my father at my side, the days and evenings hung with the jewels of the altar. Until we're at the centre, tangled perhaps, but glutted, knowing.

Now we're at the meeting of the two carpets in the church, the centre of a blue cross. The light of the mountains hazes in from the doorway to my left. The organ spins notes and words out into it, while the vaulted ceiling comes so close I could touch it.

You can't have one

You can't have one

You can't have one

Without the oth—er.

The minister's frowning helplessly at the organist's back, Tim's twisting his body around, he's searching his pockets, he's lost the ring.

You want to be my amaneunsis.

Dad couldn't have spoken. To hear, to think in this haze of noise and light, it's impossible that he spoke. As if he'd ask me to stay. To stay and paint his pictures.

Tim's coat crinkles as he searches. The minister holds up

his hand to halt Dad, his surplice sleeve falls away from his wrist. Tim's body straightens, satisfied, he's found the ring. Dad halts, loosens my arm that lies so heavily on his. He moves away from me. He's giving me up. Over my shoulder I see him sit on a pew, his legs assured in their suit trousers. I am alone. I take a slow step, pause. Take another step. I move down the tunnel of lit sound. Away from my hope, my incandescent father. Towards an ordinary life, towards The Gap. Propelled by a silly song. As if love means everything.

And then I'm running.

I painted myself as a transparency, for I was little more, rushing into the noise of light. This bride, look, you can see through her like the moon at midday. Behind are the opaque planes of her father and her lover. But for a moment the transparency is noisy, shouting as she hurls herself into the haze of light which shatters and falls like glass. As if, by running out like that, she could become free, as if freedom were like violence, as if both were just an unbridling.

See how the haze extends over the wall.

As I run through the bushland I notice that the organist has changed tunes. She's playing something more seemly from her days of shy parties:

The thirst, that from the soule doth rise,
Doth aske a drinke divine:
But might I of Jove's Nectar sup,
I would not change for thine.

Self Portrait Three

Oil on fireplace, umbrella stand,
fire surround, fire grate
irregular

Oil on carpet strip
10 ft x 6 ft

Oil on sink

Oil on twill upholstery
6 ft x 8 ft, 3 ft x 4 ft , 3 ft x 4 ft

Oil on mahogany table top
8 ft x 4 ft

Oil on lampshades
various

Oil on plaster walls and ceiling
30 ft x 25 ft, 10 ft x 12 ft, 10 ft x 12 ft

My fingers on the brush are firm though my bones creak. I lift my arm high, I gauge the angle of descent, it's his angle, not mine, it seems inert, grim and mine seems filled with promise but he breathes behind me, I must oppose but his will beats through me like a pulse, I can't oppose. I bring the brush down on the canvas all in one movement, just as he'd wish, the angle he wishes, and the brush leaves a shining trail looping like a grimace.

I step back from the easel. There's a pause. But before I turn to see his face, he's pulling his hat down over his forehead, he's taking the umbrella out of its stand. He doesn't meet my eyes. His tread on the stairs. The door opening and slamming. And now he's trudging past the windows, weighted by his overcoat, the folded umbrella swishing the paspalum, a blurred shadow dodging between his legs. I watch him till he's almost lost to view.

That's my father here, see the peevishness as he trudges away. Over the decades enclosed in his walls, I've watched our track become a road, then a street, watched the bush become shacks, houses, townhouses. I've waited and

watched. See the sky, too, watching him. It curves its
moisture around him.

He doesn't say goodbye, he never has, he's always left out
unnecessary words and now most words are unnecessary.
But he'll stand at the road's edge wondering at the particular curve of a stem heavy with a seed pod, a curve separate
from him, distinct, he'll pluck it and bring it home for me
to paint.

Vermilion trees, he'd ordered after yesterday's walk. The
vermilion leaf was blood pooling in the dry stretches of his
palm, so richly red that for a moment our faces, bent over
the leaf, were smoothed by warmth. But I begrudged him,
though vermilion leaves were everywhere, rammed in the
jar with his fan of brushes, sticking out of a teacup and
about to topple, lolling over tins, tubes, jars, pencil stubs,
charcoal stubs on his old dressing-table.

I folded my arms. The bone in my neck creaked. Vermilion leaves, I argued. That'll alter everything. He should've
said so before. Tomorrow, are the mountains to be green?
The sky yellow? Shouldn't the painting, I ask, decide for
itself?

At least when he argued back, he had to talk to me. In
these ways I make him remember me.

Today I poke vermilion shadows in the grass. But the
silence in the studio slowly makes me gentle. I lay the oily
paint on the canvas, on the roundness of oil I slide and
dream within his sketch, the outline of his authority. I paint
with something deeper than obedience, something sadder.
I'm no longer potent or impotent, I'm so deep inside his
instructions, they don't exist. And vermilion light clings
softly to the trunks of trees.

At last, I remember what hunger is. I put down the brush,
wipe paint off my hands, find bread in the studio fridge

and eat it with the fridge door still open. I pick my teeth, watching the street. Clouds scud above the grassy nature strips, but that's all.

He'll come back. It's an ancient worry, no more. To run into a room and no-one there. Only a corpse.

It's an ancient habit, this waiting for him. The next movement of his facial muscles, this might be it, the next turn of his head, that pause before the lips twist into the next sentence. I'd lower my head to hide from the brightness about to break. It is always about to break.

But in the last ten years or so, the waiting has itself become a kind of pleasure. It has its own rhythms, its own comforts. Though there's a terror underneath. That there will come a time when there is to be no more waiting. When either he will move, or I must.

The shadow of the tree hasn't reached the verandah. When it does, I'll allow myself anxiety. I paint quick short strokes, then move more smoothly. A confusion of rhythms, he'll say. Everything must, after all, be in keeping.

There's no danger to him from the town. We're forgotten, Dad and my mother and I, though our story is part of the local lore. A delivery boy once lounged on the bottom step while I held the wire door open, and I found I'd become a local story.

A murderer and his daughter used to live here, said the boy. He killed her mother. Then the daughter, she raced off into the scrub in her wedding dress. And her father raced after her with a meat axe.

Dad had rounded the corner of the house just then, back from his walk. He looked at me sharply. I saw my life as thin as a shadow fall on the long propped-up leg of the boy. And the boy, what did he see, if anything? A woman too old to flirt with, a stick of an old man with an umbrella.

He turned his eyes to a more intriguing landscape.

They're probably still out there, he'd joked. You two had better watch out.

But the interruption of memory has disquieted me. I paint too much vermilion light. The tube is almost finished. One could say it is finished. It could be put in a pocket, taken downstairs, tomorrow another could be put in a pocket, taken downstairs. The movements of a traitor, I remember, are simple. Just simple movements.

I leave the tube almost finished on the indentation in the easel shelf. But the mountains I paint are as fragile as Dad. And on the grass there's the moisture that collects in the corners of his mouth. Strange, the looseness of old men's mouths. And in the leaves, I paint the chains of time around his neck. It's enough for my life, I say aloud in the silence of his studio. It's enough, I say as I walk past the kitchen pantry and drawer. And in the night when he stalks across the studio floor above, I wake to find the words drying on my mouth. What have I to paint that is not Dad? It's enough to be his amanuensis. As I move across the canvas, I am more my father than he is.

The shadow's reached the verandah and come beyond. I look again up the street. Only two school boys, arms around each other, fighting to kick a tin. I go downstairs, peel vegetables, put on the dinner, come upstairs, look again along the street.

But he does return at last, as he always has. The door moves softly, like a caress. Everything in me slows. I listen to his step on the stairs. I don't turn to see what he has brought home for me to paint. It's perfect, this moment as he enters the studio, his hands full of what I am to paint tomorrow. It will always be like this, an accumulation of tomorrows, a layering of peace.

We don't exchange hellos, Dad and me, it doesn't matter.

It's enough that the house holds us both, the walls contain us.

I hear the clunk of the umbrella in its stand. The sighing of the coat. The compression of the sofa. The outbreath from his lips.

You've overdone the vermilion, he says. An attempt to refute.

I sit on the sofa's arm. You were gone so long, I say. I didn't think of stopping. I just wanted to please you.

You're always an extremist, he says. Either tentative, or excessive. You do nothing, or everything. You were always like that. Human nature doesn't change.

He's crossed his leg, swinging his free foot in short, sharp movements.

If only you had the promise I had, he says.

I'll rescue the painting tomorrow, I say. I wasn't trying to prove you wrong. It was the light. I should've stopped much earlier. I lost judgement.

It probably can't be rescued, he says. But his foot slows.

We breathe into the early evening, that grey hour when everything is stretched out in longing.

The dinner, I say, getting up.

I don't want my name on that painting, he says.

Then there's no point, I say.

We stare at the painting which I now see is clumsy with colour.

Except for the lower left hand corner, he says.

We look at the lower left hand corner.

It's perfect, he says. A perfect moment, those leaves. You painted them as if you've lived a long time.

In my relief, I remember every evening is like this. The condemnation. And then the easing out. And yet I forget, each time it happens his resentment feels new, appalling. A new thing that changes what has been, what will be. A rhythm at the end of every day, the dread of loss, the easing. I learn it again and again, every evening. As if I can't learn who he is. As if I don't know.

I run my finger down my nose. It's a habit of these days, these evenings. I move my finger softly, scarcely touching, and stop just above the upper lip. That's all, just down the nose to the lip. For years I didn't think about Tim, I couldn't reach back into a memory of him. There was only numbness. No glimpses, just an absence, a peculiar numbness. Then one evening when I was cowering, my finger lifted and ran down the length of my face. It was such warmth, the finger just above the cushion of air, tracing me, making me new, separate from the air, achieved, actual. The finger sculpting me. The way Tim had done when we lay naked in front of the fire.

What are you doing? Dad had asked.

Remembering, I'd said.

I take his coat, his warmth in it. I stroke it.

What have you brought for me to paint? I ask.

Perhaps you're impatient with what I want you to paint, says Dad. Perhaps that's the problem.

Carrying Dad's warm coat, I walk past the painting. The vermilion glows. In the gloom of the room, the vermilion has drained the other colours and floats by itself.

What else is there to say but what I say? Dad demands.

I hang up the coat, walk towards the stairs.

Nothing, I say.

It's an echo ricocheting in the staircase.

There's nothing but what you have to say. Nothing else.

I hear him moving on the sofa.

I've brought something home, he says.

I turn at the top of the stairs.

News, he says.

His back is to me, a sphinx, a ghost.

I met someone, he says.

Who? I ask.

Someone who's interested in art, he says. And my work.

From the township? I wonder.

She's got money, he says. She might buy some paintings.

She, I repeat, and walk down into a new echo.

She visits us. She's a raucous intruder.

Ohh, she says, as soon as she comes in. I know what your paintings are about.

She clasps her hands in front of her, she blinks in excitement, she contrives to look up at Dad although she's his height.

The righteousness of power. Am I right?

Dad, following, his hands behind his back. I was not expecting him to trail after her. I was not expecting his smile.

Such pride, she says.

She's running to the next painting, high heels clicking, plastic raincoat crunching as she bends to look.

And the helplessness, so, so . . .

What about the helplessness?

My voice is shrill. They both turn to me, look back to the paintings. She speaks to Dad, the artist, shutting me out by the shine on her raincoat.

Do you think one dreams when one looks at paintings?

She's breathless for an answer.

I mean, if they're, they're, her hands twirl, come together, clasp each other for strength, if they speak a truth?

Dad clenches his hands behind his back. Perhaps, he says.

She glances back at me, she can hear the bones in my neck move.

When I say dream, I mean, while one is awake, looking.

Some deeper part of the mind is, shall we say, sluiced by darker waters.

Perhaps, says Dad.

You know, she breathes. Her eyes are secret hiding places, caves, she invites him in. You know, she breathes again.

She runs to the next painting.

So that one is looking at the painting, and at oneself, and negotiating.

You don't mind, she throws a smile over a shining shoulder, you don't mind my being forward in my opinions. Speaking my mind. I mean, an artist . . .

Not at all, says Dad.

Such meaningful work, she says.

Dad glances away from the promise in the glittering caves. And sees me, hovering.

My daughter paints too.

Molly sinks into the sofa, the plastic mac whistles.

Two artists in one room, she says. Do you think I might have a cup of tea?

At the other end of the studio, at the sink, Dad is there above the rush of water.

Get the teacups, he says. With saucers. There used to be some downstairs. Lady-like ones. With flowers.

His voice booms down the length of the room.

We both paint. One painting, two artists. I tell my daughter what to do.

I don't look in the direction of his voice. I square my shoulders. The creak in the neck. I sniff. For twenty years now I have painted his paintings. And signed them. With his signature.

The china cabinet has been in the hall so long that it's part of the shape of the house, its nature, a protrusion to walk

around. Only the drift of voices down the stairs and
through the open door makes me pull at the catch. It's stuck
with age. I walk to the end of the hall, pull the light cord,
come back, work the catch. The voices have an imperative,
the catch obeys it, the door comes open. It hangs lopsid-
edly. Dad must've neglected to mend a hinge forty years
ago. I prop up the door. A yellowed label from a furniture
shop has spindly, elegant writing.

Deliver by

The date has long gone.

Deliver to

Someone has written in purple ink, perhaps it wasn't
purple then.

Mrs Montrose.

With a doodle after, a circle within circle, as if the shop
assistant became lost in cogitation before tearing the label
off a pad and sticking it inside the door. I'm on my knees
on the carpet in the glare of light with my mother's name
and the shop assistant's doodle. Did he doodle as he
watched my mother walking away high-heeled down a
shiny floor, had she said something that made him daydream, or was he just waiting for his morning tea? I touch
the name, I touch only a yellow crinkling label. And it
comes to me that I've always thought about why she had
to stay with Dad. I've never thought about why she had to
leave.

Here are the cups, upside down and crackling on dusty
saucers. Blue-and-grey flowers and gold rims. Dad remembers the flowers. What else is in his memory?

Fire leaps in my stomach and is gone. I lift each cup and
saucer individually, carry each out to the kitchen. Dust black-
ens the sink water. It's a desecration, this washing away of the
past. And afterwards on the tea-towel are cobwebs.

*

Molly discovers another cobweb, wet and persistent on the handle of a cup. She drinks out of one of the studio mugs instead. Its thick rim makes her bold.

I see a contradiction in your work, she says to Dad.

I see with surprise that her mouth is pursed, the lipstick clings to cracks in her lips now that the tea has taken the surface gloss.

Dad moves quickly to her side.

These paintings are about power, she says. But these other paintings here, you mute power, you make helplessness triumph. This dead bird, this hopeful landscape. One expects a resurrection.

Dad leans against the wall.

The work, he says, spans a long time.

Ah, she says. The simpler statements would be the early work. And the later work, the more complex.

Too complex, says Dad. In the later work, that's where I've been helped by my daughter. I'm often disappointed.

Ah, she says, into the long silence that follows. Don't be. Don't be. No, don't be.

I trace the line from my forehead to just above my mouth.

The earlier work, she says, is so insistent that one rebels. Resists. While the later work carries its own rebellion within itself. Either way, one doesn't feel peaceful afterwards. And isn't that what you both meant to do? Disturb?

Yes, says Dad. Of course. Yes.

Artists, she says, hold us all in their hands.

The plastic mac laughs in triumph.

Such wonderful, inspired, sacred hands. Sacred. May I— she takes Dad's hands, lifts them, kisses them. And blows a kiss to mine.

Would you like, says Dad, another cup of tea?

As I return from the kitchen, her back is turned to me. There's a huddle of paintings leaning against the sofa near her handbag. I mouth: Is she buying them? He ignores me.

Dad refuses to have the light on, refuses dinner. Often I eat alone in the dark, my cutlery clinking against his thoughts. He asks me not to swallow. I leave the plates on the table and sit beside him. Slowly the bush invades the studio. Shadows clamber over the floor, the walls. The sofa is as pale, as mysterious as the moon. A cricket outside the window however is familiar, obstinate.

It's your hubris, he says.

She didn't know what she was talking about, I say.

You are always combative, he says. That's why none of the later paintings work.

I'd only be able to follow you more closely, I say, if I were you.

We sit, creatures of the night. It's always like this between us now. Me, creaking, unsure, touching my nose, defiant, placating. Him, resentful, needy. We run, we snarl, follow each other's tracks, hunt each other down, we sink exhausted, circle around each other, sleep.

Sometimes I think of Auntie, her lips quivering. Dumped. I knew then, I know now, how to wait. How not to be dumped.

Molly's bought more paintings than everyone put together for the last twenty years, says Dad.

She bought very good paintings, I say. The shame is, she wouldn't know how good they are.

It's pitch black. The moon has gone. The room is chilly. I may have been asleep. Suddenly his voice is there, as urgent, plaintive as a trumpet.

I feel I've been wandering around lost for a long time. And now someone's come and found me. Now I can start again.

I'm awake. The cricket has stopped.

*

Dad goes for walks, I say to Molly. Long walks. And he's only just left.

I'm happy to wait, she says.

I'll tell him you visited, I say.

I begin to shut the door. But she's not daunted by me, she stays where she is.

I've got too much work to stand chatting, I say.

Her hair is pulled away from her neck, baring a thick lushness like the flesh of Arum lilies. Ripped apart, they leave only stretches of nectar threads in the hands.

I'll curl up in a corner somewhere, she says.

Like a cat, she slides past me.

I rattle my brush against the sides of the turps jar but she keeps turning the pages of the magazine she's brought.

She's one of those people who suck fingers loudly to turn pages, denting the gloss of the advertisements, but peering. As if they could save her life, I'll report to Dad.

You keep breaking away from my outline, he'd said this morning. If you don't want to comply, don't pretend.

So I lay the oils on respectfully. Tonight we'll sit together in the floating twilight listening to the comfort of each other's stomachs.

She noisily turns a page. I glare, but she's engrossed. Her neck curves, a man would want to touch that curve. To see if the skin would part silently at the insistence of fingers.

Sometimes in front of his easel I pretend I'm Dad. I breathe in, not with the chest as a woman does, but with the stomach, flaring the muscles there, rounding them. My belt expands, contracts. Sweat rises from my confidence, I'm pleased at my stench. I'm no-one's pleasure, only mine. Like him.

She turns another page. Her shoes lie pigeon-toed on the floor. Her feet are crossed on the sofa arm. Just us girls, I remember the phrase from schooldays. Crimson toe-nails painted to appease. And the skirt demure over the knees lest anyone should enter the room.

A page crackles again into my concentration. You test me, he'd said. The air was breaking with words.

You are forever contradicting.

Sometimes despair rots me, deep in the abdomen, rots like a carcass in the bush noisy with flies.

I've given you my life, I'd said. What more do you want?

You're waiting me out, he'd said. Waiting for your will to take me over. Give up. Or don't pretend to paint for me.

But when the air seals over, we both know he's the one pretending. I am his arms, hands, fingers. He wouldn't amputate himself. See Dad, how I submit, stroking the canvas, almost not touching, always within your boundaries. One hand calming the other I glide on oil, I caress, I glide away.

She has begun to hum. She doesn't see my glare, her eyes are gobbling the advertisements in the magazine, they quiver, they swallow. She pulls up her skirt to scratch her thigh through her nylons. She's noisy in nylons. Pointed toes, thin legs, a dancer's legs, stalking music under a ridiculous tutu.

You must leave, I'll say. Now.

I inhale, about to speak.

Having a rest, are you? she asks. She's looking up.

I came wanting to have another look at the paintings. And a chat. And to show how I've hung the ones I bought, she says.

She digs in her bag, produces a photo, holds it up. And keeps holding it up, so I must walk over to look.

There's still a space on the wall, she says. Open spaces make me lonely. One more painting should do the trick.

Her room, I see, is furnished excessively, noisily.

Dad will tell you he's not an interior decorator, I say.

She smiles lipsticked lips.

You've never married, have you, she says.

There's no question in her voice.

I'm embarrassed by lack into replying.

There's no time, I say. This house. Dad's needs. I am, after all, his amanuensis.

The absence when I think of Tim. When I force myself to remember his face, the shapes eventually come together, but it's the face of somebody else. The clerk at the post office, if there was someone to write a letter to. A man driving past as I walk down the road to the butcher's. The gaze of a boy on a motor bike at a girl. Later I clutch the meat packages on the creek bank and watch his buttocks rise and fall, lifting high and settling into the furred creases of his legs. That night, and for many nights afterwards, my hand between my legs, I couldn't choose who to be; him, burrowing into her white viscous pleasure, her, glutted, with no empty spaces.

You must leave, I say to Molly.

I didn't mean to distress you, she says. The way you paint, speak, move, dress, everything about you is so chaste. You didn't mind me asking, did you? I mean, it's an ordinary question.

I paint on.

You're not sure there's anyone inside your dress, she says. And you don't want anyone else to wonder, either.

I paint where he wanted, the magenta, the cyanine blue, discords to set the nerves jangling. I prefer earth colour days, with yellow ochre and Indian red drying like dust in the throat, in the trees, turning everything into a millenium of stone.

I want to tell you why I'm really here, she says suddenly.

She's standing beside me, urgently close.

I think we understand each other, she says. It happens sometimes between women, immediately. Whereas men and women, they must play. At least in the beginning. If not always.

You're standing in my light, I say.

I'm plastering paint on the canvas, straight on, straight out of the tubes, no time for the mediation of the palette, her smell around me, what is it, lavender and onions, this woman of contradictions with her dancer's legs and her plastic mac. I need the thickness of paint, I'm quick, bold, sharp, I'll thin it later, wipe it off, when she sits down I'll duplicate his sketch more accurately.

Her lips are parted with eagerness. She's composing the story of her life, I see, in the hope that I find it extraordinary. I've heard women at the shops like this, hurrying towards the bargains, but I've looked into their bags afterwards, and there are only the disappointed packages.

When you made the leaf brighter you changed the geometry, she says. So that things seem more subtle to me when I look away. Familiar things. My hand, for example.

She has a plump white hand without lines, the fat fills it so well.

You flout, she says. You flout.

I've been breathing at her rate. I hold my breath, breathe my own breath.

That's your strength, she says. And you have strength, you know. You don't know it, but you are strong.

I'm holding onto the brush as if it's an anchor, essential but perhaps capricious.

A small physical change can wreak havoc in the mind, she says. Or offer salvation. I've always been excited by things that haven't been completely explored. When I was a child I kept hoping that one morning one of the houses in the street would disappear. I'd go out of my front door and hope the house would be gone. Because only when things become mysterious does there seem to be a possibility of meaning. But artists don't think that, do they? she's pleading.

There's a mole on her lush white neck. I paint it into the painting. For good measure, I paint in her neck as well.

Then when I had a child of my own, she says, I lost my awe. I thought: I can be at the centre, pushing. And when I held him afterwards, he traced the shape of my face with his tiny finger. As if he was wondering what I am.

I make the mole bigger, a reef bursting out of a calm moonless sea.

That's why I came to art, she says. That's why I'm here.

You're hoping to find what's possible in you, I say. I'm panting.

What's inevitable. What must emerge, I add.

You know, she breathes as she breathed to Dad. You know. How I envy you and your father. Pushing at the centre all the time, every day. Making things appear, disappear. And doing it—she throws back her head so there's a further expanse of white neck—together.

I'm rescued by that word.

It's not like that, I say. I'm only an amanuensis. There are some days when I hope, like everyone else. Most of the time I just keep inside the boundaries.

She twitches, smiles her bright smile.

Can't you do that, and still explore? she asks.

Have you thought, I ask, that all you might get from art is paintings?

I like her, her noise, whatever she threatens. I put down the brush.

Have you thought, she asks, of painting by yourself?

Dad glides in so quietly back from his walk that at first I think it's only his shadow.

The problem with painting by myself, the act of it, is its presumption. An act of such will, patterning the chaos. An act of violence, making it hold my imaginings.

But since she spoke, I've been looking at my hands. They're not pretty it's true, there's a lot of spare flesh pulling this way and that, I'm embarrassed to see them in a portrait, not that there's much of that these days or even that Dad and I consider them my hands, but that's the point. They're mine. My hands. My. I. They're joined to my invisible body but they're visible. I'm holding them out in front of me now. In the blur that's me, there they are, hard-edged.

I watch them stir white sauce so it doesn't lump. Slide new elastic through the waist of his underpants. Scrub the bath with cleaning powder. Carry his tray. Paint inside his outlines. I begin to think: if there's my hands, there's also me.

I steal his paints again. Cadmium yellow, cerulean blue, alizarin crimson, viridian green, vermilion. They're not jewels, not an incantation. Just one stolen colour a week, a basic palette.

There's sewing machine oil to mix with the stolen paints. There are no brushes, no canvases. But there are surfaces, many hidden surfaces. Cupboard doors in the kitchen downstairs where surely he won't pry again. The insides of doors. If only I open the doors and begin.

In the day I look at them, doors I haven't dared open all through my youth and middle age, and at night they creak in my dreams.

You have rings around your eyes, says Dad as I clear the plates from the table.

Molly has come to dinner.

He's right, she says to me.

You work so hard, you're not getting enough rest.

I don't scrape the plates, I stack them on top of each other, bones and all, and hurry out of the studio.

I choose a cupboard door near the stove because I walk past it five times a day, breakfast, morning tea, lunch, afternoon tea and dinner. The lino around it is cracked with heel prints. My heel prints. My heel prints give me courage.

The silence in the night when there are things to be done not connected with darkness is a silence writhing with whispers. I kneel on a sheet of newspaper. The lino is cold under my knees. I tug at the door handle. The door comes open with a crack. There's nothing inside but cobwebs and a daddy-long-legs and it meanders away good humouredly.

I take the lid off the jar of turps. It's settled to orange, this turps, from the washings of colours upstairs. I drop the lid, it clangs on the lino. A sound like that, its enigma, seems substantial. I bend the door back on its hinges. I hold the past in scatterings of dirt. Not all the past, but enough to make the rest less daunting.

I'll start tomorrow night, I say. But I don't start. I darn socks, polish door handles, wash to the bottom of the laundry basket, go to bed early, need more and more sleep. I must get all the tasks done. I must concentrate on my work with him. I must let the primer dry thoroughly.

I'm worn out, I say to Dad and Molly, who's stayed to dinner every night this week.

You do too much, says Molly. On the go, all the time.

I make palette knives from kitchen knives, I make brushes from meat skewers, rags, and my own hair. I run out of excuses.

*

Have you ever noticed how assertive paint is?

By myself, I can't make a mark.

I watch them come down the road, his hand gallant at her elbow, his eyes anxious on the pebbles, his arm ready to hold the wind from her hair. How close together are his fingers on her sleeves, unwilling that the material of her blouse should slip out of his grasp. She wobbles and glints in her excited high heels. And his umbrella flaps by his side. It's not raining, but the sky threatens and he's unrolled it. Unrolled his umbrella. Until this moment I've doubted. But there it is, black, flapping, indisputable.

See how I've painted them, Molly and Dad, two tiny figures leaning on each other in hope, while the great wild jagged cliffs rage around them.

I know by that unrolled umbrella that it's too late for me, too late. I've behaved as if I had not these forty years but a million, as if I could sleep forever, murmuring not today, it can't be today, tomorrow I'll take action, let me sleep now.

Dad and I could still be standing together at the windows on the cliff's edge, just the two of us, it would still be me he'd invite into the mystery. If only I hadn't flouted, that was her word, flouted. If only, I say as I walk around the house listening in the stillness to the dragging of my feet. If only. If only. If only.

Oh, I was so proud, thinking I knew better than Auntie and Mum how to wait. Dumped. I remember Auntie's lips. Before the epiphany has begun, I've been dumped.

But I caused it, didn't I, by flouting. All those times he wanted a tree with a spine of light, a rock more abrupt, a pool more languid, I gave him, let me say it, disobedience.

Oh I was luxurious in disobedience, no wonder he helps her off with her coat as if he fears she might disappear, that he might be left with nothing but empty coat sleeves. It would've been so easy to give him his languid pool, his abrupt rock, his lit tree. It wasn't so very important to me. But I confronted him with mockery.

Why should I serve him, I'd raged, and walked into the village and looked at young men on motor bikes, hoping they'd look back at me, just to feel the heat from their faces. Why should I wait, I'd raged. But what was I waiting for, what had I been waiting for, all these years? Why was I no better than a child wandering in the grey bush, unable to formulate a question? And now it's too late.

I fan his brushes, tidy the tubes, neaten the doilies, scrub the verdigris in the sink. I notice dust on the window sill. Too late. He has stood here every morning framed by my unconcern.

If only I could say, beg, plead with him, those words I know, the words of submission, if I could say to her: give me more time. There's something Dad and I must acknowledge, something I must do. If I can think what it is.

I remember the night I'd blurted out, after an hour scribbling a rehearsal in the kitchen, an hour torn constantly into pieces and thrown into the garbage, I'd blurted out her faults to him over dinner. As if she was the problem. His hands shovelling in the cold meat, his fingers greasy with hunger. She clings to art as if it's a rope over a white-teethed chasm, I said. She rhapsodises only so she can't hear the silence, I said. She's a child, I said. But in my anger I'd burnt the chops, so black I had to throw them away, and speak over slices of cold meat. He hates cold meat. I knew it was untimely, as always my timing with him is wrong, I knew it from the moment he saw the chilly meat with its grim festoon of fat. But I couldn't stop, I'd waited too long, anger crammed up my throat, my lips were knots of words before his knife screamed across the plate.

It's extraordinary, this loss, it catches me like a bone in the wrong place when I'm passing milk for teacups or peeling carrots or painting his canvases. Yesterday, signing one, I heaved a grief so deep I had to stop, between the E and the O of Geoffrey, I had to stop and sit. But where was there to sit? Only on his sofa. I sat instead on the stairs, head in my lap, and let the stairwell echo, until I could imagine there was someone weeping with me.

Sometimes I follow them on their walks, deep in the scrub while they walk on footpaths. I watch his hand as it moves at her waist. I am his hand. I am her waist. I watch them shuffle feet so they're in step. And if they look around, there are only ant hills.

You're working slowly, says Dad, watching me paint inside his outlines. But I won't complain. You're getting the hang of it at last.

He rubs his fingers, clenched, against my cheek. An unfamiliar gesture, one recently learned.

After all these years, eh?

He sits down on the sofa. I see with dread he's smiling, contained. His shoulders are sure and confident.

Lately I've been thinking that I should get back to doing my own painting again, he says.

He plumps the sofa next to him, where I am to sit. But I stand looking down at his sureness.

Why? My voice is as thin as the evening light.

You could get on with the housework, uninterrupted. Molly says you're looking worn out, and it's true.

He's still patting the sofa for me.

But if we take you off the painting, it'll be a waste of all the time and trouble I've put into training you. Now that you're just beginning to come good.

Now on the road around the cliffs, yellow coreopsis twist sleepily at their passing. My eye moves up from the trees gripped by the darkened valley below, from Molly and Dad pulled to the ground by the sticks and pebbles on the road, my eye rears up the sheer sandstone cliff face, my eye is foolish, it discounts a millenium of wind and sand and sun, it pleads: let the slopes go on, up, beyond, reach out, on, on, rip open that blue ceiling, if only they could, ah then. But the cliffs are lopped off, sudden, mocking. And between the cliff tops and that haze of blue light the space hears me, struggles for me, teeters, regains itself, lunges out, falters, falls back in disappointment, becomes The Gap.

In the moonlit clearing, Dad's shouts flicker.

The shadows are sharper than in the day, he calls.

He whirls on his heels, to prove. An old man with his trouser legs flaring. I scratch my bare arm where a bush has prickled. So he contorts himself into strange shapes, a ladder, a kite, a cross. I walk on in the uncertain air.

The neighbours will wonder, I say.

He holds back twigs so my face isn't scratched. As he does for Molly. I stretch my lips into a smile.

Dance with me, he says on the road glittering with stones.

Once I longed for something like this, so close we might mingle eyes. One of his arms around my waist, the other pointing to the moon. Against trees cartwheeling between shadow and silver. Beyond the clump of coreopsis at the end of the street, a stone arcs into stars four thousand light years away and down, down into the trees that carpet the gully.

Slower, I beg.

Not since his violent days have we been so close.

But he grabs me and I'm whirling, pinioned on his hip and whirling, dizzy with tree trunks and dust and his grunts and our shadows that leap from the road, into us, past and over the ridge of the cliff like stones.

Stop, I shout.

But he's watching the picture we make on the moonlit road, the rag doll flung on his determined hip, and for a while my nausea belongs to someone else, not me, I watch with him the rag doll that's me with legs splayed out like sticks. Then the nausea comes back to me and I'm in the bushes choking and hunched, with Dad and the moon beyond. I can't see him, but I hear the exhilaration of him. I hear it between one spasm of vomit and the next, the promise he makes about the future, something he'll give, something he'll make possible, cure, seal away. He catches me in my despair, he always has, he lifts me up, he makes a promise so bright that it tracks across the mind's darkness like a star. All my life, I haven't dared look around.

He leaves.

The vomit on the grass at my knees is spangled by moonlight into streamers. He's gone to switch on his studio lights, he always eludes. Molly reaches out to touch him every day, I see her reach as she pours milk into his tea. He's battled all his life, it's been an odyssey for him, she says, and I see how rigorously her lips smile, the lines guarding each end of her mouth in case of disappointment. Don't reach out to him, I want to shout to her. You'll find nothing in your hand. He's as spellbinding, as insubstantial as moonlight.

A breeze stings my bared knees with dust. Here on my knees, if I knew what the promise was, if I could see how little it was in words so reductive, receding so fast, I could spit it out of me, in one fierce free moment I could spit it

out into the black trees and walk away. Away from Dad.
The wind writhes up from the gully and covers me in moonlight white as a shroud.

*I was in a painted world, as still as one of the portraits my
father had painted of me, so still that you looked and said:
It's only the tension that holds it there, nothing is locked
by line, it's in a state of becoming, it has its own movement,
which will suddenly burst out. That stillness is fragile, at
any moment it will be action. That's why this portrait
seems so still. Why I did.*

What's that down here? The click of a front door at dawn.

The sound drops onto the floorboards I've polished till they
gleam with appeasement. It's very early for him to go out.
He's always been trenchant opening doors. I remember as a
child, doors for me widened with fear under the force of his
hand. I'd cower under the tall door frame until he threatened
to leave forever down the distance of the garden path.

Pebbles crunch on frost brittle ground. A laugh, but it's
smothered like guilt. He's not alone. Loss keeps entering
me, as appalling as death. In the long ages between the
footsteps of two people, I make myself think it through: it's
early, she wouldn't have visited him so early, she must've
stayed the night.

The gate on its hinges, the dawn dark with rustles.
Another spurt of smothered laughter, full of the hiss of
whispers.

Mornings have been for a long time soft with bird calls
and a fresh fold of the bed sheets to burrow into. And
perhaps the wind coming up the valley will anaesthetise the
day. This dawn is not like that.

The downpipe, rusted and glum with age, blocks my

view. They're coming into sight, walking slowly to her car, walking like ghosts, insubstantial. From this distance it's a silent film, not jerky but sadly drifting, as if they could dissolve into the mountains, into each other. Only the dawn breeze in my ears. They reach the car, pause, she takes her hand out of his, unlocks the door, holds it open, waits, looks at him, she's incomplete. He prods her into the seat, picks up a trail of her skirt and tucks it in, shuts the door. Distance, like a dream, muffles the slam. She unwinds the window, her arms reach out, they reach out like branches grasping the sky. He stands where he is. Her arms wave. He looks up the road, down it. Her arms retreat. She winds up the window but a tiny triangle of her long green woollen scarf catches at the top of the window. It continues to flap at Dad. A reverse, a turn. He holds up his hand in a formal salute or a dismissal. Much further away, I hear thunder, like groans. And under, she dissolves into the hills raw with rain. With a tiny tuft of green scarf still pleading with Dad.

Gradually I hear his footsteps, his feet slurping in puddles, the gate banging wetly, proclaiming. And then the door, he pulls it so quickly behind him.

Is that what he was like when he courted Mum?

Everyday I watch her face as he leaves the room. He touches her shoulder as he leaves, perhaps only to steer himself around the corner of the table. She doesn't look at her shoulder, at the spot he touched, but all her body is looking, I know.

She turns her brightness to me.

Your father is a great man.

There are always dishes to stack, tablecloths to shake. I watch myself shaking the tablecloth.

He is, I say, many things.

*

On most nights I struggle with my canvases, which are the cupboard doors. At first I arrange objects on the kitchen table, a flamboyant still-life of onions, apples, a pumpkin, the iron. But flamboyance intimidates me. So, onions and a pumpkin on the breadboard. Onions on a breadboard. An onion.

I stare at the onion for several nights. I won't paint just a glimpse of an onion, I'll paint its whole as I know it and I know about onions, I've cut them all my life, my fingers stenched, my eyes stinging while he crunches them raw, salt-encrusted. It's not merely an onion I'm painting, this onion will be a metaphor for all that I've known, its shine, shadows, smoothness, its glistening crispness, the white way it burrows into itself, all this I know and will paint. Into this painting of an onion I'll paint memories, chinks of light and stretches of shadow and eyes and the mouth of death and firelight on skin and the shape of rooms and memories and voices, the noise of years and the long white bony stillness of death. So that later, if someone chanced to walk by they would say: Ah, I see what she means. This painting will be, in its own way, a portrait of my life. If only I could stop the pounding of my heart. The way it twists into my stomach when I hold the brush. The way my mind whispers: This will be the moment at last.

Every night my heart pounds, I hold my chest to stop it, every night I struggle with the metaphor of the onion. When one door gets over-painted, I work on the next door, the next, the next. I paint onions, I paint them out. But the onions resist me, they refuse to contain my meanings.

After a month I shut the doors on a row of painstakingly accurate onions, as opaque as stones.

Every morning that she stays to breakfast I stand near him in his warmth. Every night my hands have been cold.

Dad, I say one morning, let's paint that night when we danced outside.

His eyeballs are large in the lids, blank white spaces that curve away from me. Molly's spoon scrapes in her bowl.

It's not a fit subject, he says.

So I show him that it is, there, with a knife amongst the checks on the tablecloth, scattering toast crumbs. Which Molly brushes from her blouse with meticulous fingers. After she's been with Dad at night, her breasts huddle together.

Perhaps, says Dad.

Molly suggests another cup of tea. I need more room on the table to describe, moving the cereal boxes. The splintered moonlight. The ricocheting figures. The landscape full of secrets.

Molly brushes her blouse again, it's silk, the silk whistles under her fingernails. Her knuckles dimple prettily to hold the plates. On top, the toast rack teeters. Dad pretends it's falling and needs to be caught, the table-cloth scrunches. I straighten out my sketch. Her buttocks under her leather skirt are demandingly muscular.

One day, says Dad, we should paint Molly walking away.

I move my chair closer to him, his amanuensis. And speak softly, so he must lean forward to hear. It's irresistible to him, the hope of the next painting. I straighten my fingers, he straightens his, I curve mine, he curves his and nods, we're a continuum of each other and his wrist bone appears and disappears below his jumper cuff. I've always known the shape of his hands.

She comes back to the doorway, watching us.

What's that over there where the palette knife has pulled the paint apart? I suppose you could say it looks like a scream.

*

Broken china still slithering on the studio floor, one plate reaches the sink pipe, spins and is still. A table knocked over as Dad runs. He's cradling her, she's burying herself in him.

I just lost balance, the floor's so slippery, everything's so cramped up here.

He's hushing her, cradling, soothing.

I'm piecing crockery together uselessly, getting the broom.

You're trying to break someone's neck.

I turn, Dad's face is red blotches.

That's what you're up to. The amount of polish lately. The floor's like an ice-rink. You're trying to kill someone.

It burns, the elation that hits the stomach. I find his eyes. They don't waver at the mention of death.

She's uncoiling from his arms, he helps her up, she adjusts her clothes, pulls her blouse in at the belt.

It's so cramped up here, when there's a perfectly good kitchen downstairs.

He's shaping her face as he brushes back her hair. As if his hands could form everything, everything, the house, the sky, the air, right from the beginning. I remember Tim's hands.

Can't I use the kitchen downstairs? she asks him. She's pouting, a little girl who might cry.

Leave the housework to Frances, he says. That's not what you're here for.

I see how her hands dangle, as toast crumbs crunch under her feet.

This morning two birds lay under the studio windows. I found them in the early sunshine, their bodies already cold. They must have been flying together, perhaps migrating, and in the dark night crashed blindly into the wall of glass.

Their wings seared the morning with colour, emerald, vermilion, gold and Prussian blue, their bodies were heavy with the precision of death but their wings were still raised in a blur of hope.

Where were we? he asks.

He comes back to the table after comforting Molly. I'm still sitting where I was and he must come back, even though he pierces the floor with his sharp heels. There is always the next painting for the artist and the amanuensis. His hands lie on the table, heavy, blunt, I must nudge them to complete the outline of the moon. And suddenly I know that I am ready, that it must be now, until now I've opposed, no, flouted, in revenge for what I've forgotten, some ancient fury, but now I could focus his vision, could paint for him better than if I were him. It would be him painting in me. I know what he hates, what he hungers for. Love, what is it, only the lull between paintings, and for him and Molly, a twitch of the body. He must come back to me because I give birth to him.

I know what his heavy hands have to paint. The righteousness of the strong. The pathetic yielding of the weak. To him that's absolute, a law of nature, truth. The landscape outside, the landscape inside, he must create it over and over again. I've always known what his landscapes are about. I've always been inside his landscape.

When the house is in darkness, I hear her walking down the stairs. I wait for the distant click of the front door. There's a scraping instead, the intimate sound of bare feet. She's in the kitchen, she's come in the stairs door. She's staring at cupboards. Her eyes are wide.

I didn't want to wake you, she says. I just needed something to help me sleep.

This is my part of the house, I say.

Just some ovaltine or cocoa, she says.

No-one comes through that door but me, I say.

She pulls her dressing gown tightly around her. That way she looks chastened. I get cocoa down from a shelf, push it at her.

You'll find everything else you need upstairs, I say.

She doesn't take the cocoa.

Is that sensible, she says. I mean, I'll wake your father.

She's looking around the kitchen.

It's only an ordinary kitchen, she says. There's nothing to hide.

I switch out the light.

Your eyes will adjust in a minute, I say. And there's plenty of moonlight to see your way back.

She feels for the cocoa in my hand. But stays, a dark shape on the kitchen floor.

I don't know what to do, she says.

Feel your way along the wall, I say. Just keep walking. You'll get to the stairs eventually.

It's not that, she says in the darkness. That's not what I'm uncertain of.

She's no longer bright, noisy, her knuckles clutch the cocoa as if it could tell her something.

You resent me, she says.

No, I say. Not exactly.

It makes me shudder, the cold lino or her white knuckles.

Everything's so precarious here, I say.

You're afraid I'll take your place, she says.

No, I say again.

They need so much definition, these elusive things.

I have my place, I say. I've worked that out. With great difficulty. Many losses. It's taken all my life. I'm safe now. I've made choices and I'm safe in it. But you must work out your place, without encroaching on me. It's critical.

You make it sound like life and death, she says, trying out a laugh in her voice.

You know about Mum? I ask.

It was an accident. A long time ago, she says. That's in the past.

But everything slips into the past immediately, I say. So we're always in the past. It's all we've got.

Her voice cuts against mine.

I'm keeping you out of bed, she says.

She turns, walks out of the kitchen. My eyes have adjusted. I watch her pale hand on the wall, stretched out flat, the palm clinging, sliding, pausing, clinging, sliding, pausing to take her weight and her uncertainty, all the way to the stairs door.

But Dad and I, we paint the picture of the dance. And I wonder that I ever dared call myself his amanuensis before, now that I most truly am. Every day Dad talks over with me what I'm to paint, Molly listening, her feet drawn up on the sofa, breathing softly, intent. He talks and I nod, when he inclines his head I do, when he nods I do, yes, I say, yes, that's it exactly, oh yes. Just as he wishes.

There's no argument in me, I'm not flouting. What he believes, I will believe, that power is righteous, inevitable, that the weak are paltry, envious, mean-spirited. I wonder that I never saw it before, the years gone past now seem like a lie. But perhaps I could only come to this point slowly, I had to spend my life learning him like a country, the rivers, mountains, plains, cliffs, I had to learn how to walk here.

You've wasted a lot of time, he says. Yours, and mine. I could've done wonders if you'd come to your senses sooner.

But I suspect he prefers that I've taken so long, he speaks

with a smile, his smiles have always been so rare. As if I've travelled everywhere else recalcitrant to spite him, and now, begging forgiveness, I've at last come home.

Day after day I become him, I become his painting. I'm enthralled when they're not in the house, I encourage their walks, I'm happiest at that moment when I see them moving away from me down the road. The air glows with my alone-ness. Then I'm most truly Dad, no-one can limit or mock me, my head seethes with shapes that have never been there before, colours and shadows startle, I'm proud, victorious. I paint in short sharp strokes, fierce on the palette, abrupt on the canvas, I jab to highlight the triumph of trees, leaves, limbs; the grass cowers, bushes reel in terror, rocks ingratiate. I'm not painting a landscape, I'm painting him. I stand as he does, one leg conceding weight to another, confident, deter-mined, insistent. I throw back my head to watch the whole canvas, my eye is a glittering transparency. When I stop to change the turps I find my knees locked, my jaws jammed together. Once I catch myself gritting my teeth. And in the evening I feel my hand. For a few minutes it's numb on my wrist, slowly it recovers, becomes mine.

But my mind, that doesn't come back to me, it stays in his, numbed, not returning, belonging to the paint, to him.

You must be strong to concede so much.

I look up to Molly's voice.

I don't know what you're talking about, I say.

She smiles.

Nevertheless it's given him a new lease of life, she says. Whatever it's doing to you.

When they come back home he spends minutes in silence in front of the easel, he doesn't unbutton his coat, he won't let Molly put the umbrella in the stand.

You've almost got it right, he says to me. You're almost there.

His praise inflames me with ambition, I walk out on the cliff road, I take my steps as he does, I imagine Molly by my side. I look back at the house balanced on the cliff edge, his house, I look back at his windows and he's there, a small figure towering above the silent valley. I lift my hand in a wave, he doesn't wave back, he doesn't need to acknowledge me, he still has no need of me after all these years. And I know, I see a landscape the way he sees it. To him, that tree is not leaning randomly, to him the crook of its trunk gestures in begging; those cliffs chose not to align themselves, to him, they rebel, but tomorrow they'll erode, punished. The balance of strength between those rock faces cannot be sustained, that's what Dad would think, he'd believe one must give precedence to the other. To him, the red waratahs are impertinent, they struggle for differentiation from the grey bush, unsettling its equilibrium but, see, already their petals loosen, they'll fall. The valley below is held in a hush, orderly, accommodating, acquiescent. Even the stand of gum trees is arranged in decorum. And the pebbles are silenced.

Two days later he's gripping my shoulders.

It's as if I painted it, he says. As if you're me.

I sit close to him on the sofa, we laugh like children, his umbrella tumbles on the floor, his coat is at my feet. I can scarcely eat dinner for excitement, and he can scarcely eat for talking, he has new ideas for our future paintings, paintings that require months, years of work together, he and I together, he makes sketches in the air and I follow the trails of his fingers and breathe, yes, oh yes.

Sometimes I hear Dad and Molly as I paint, there's a new

note in her voice, I listen to his voice cutting into hers and hers sliding under, I turn to see the muscles moving in her face as she stares at him. I think: She believes because she fears her disbelief.

And then one day she's pleading across the bowls of soup.

I'm painting now, she says. You two have inspired me.

Her laugh plummets. Dad spits grains of barley onto his spoon and bangs them out on the rim of his plate. I see it's a necklace that could choke. He doesn't appear to have heard her.

I'm doing it with my hands, she says. It's so physical.

She shakes her hands above her head.

I stare at the soup till she insists on enlisting my smile. I wish I'd thought to skim the fat. Rainbows in it wink at us all. She ignores our silence.

I said to myself, now's the time. Now I have two artist friends. But I'm too old to learn about brushwork. When there are such experts. Besides, this way seems so human.

I think of her arms twisting out of the car window.

But Dad cuts rounds of bread only for himself with his short knife. Her eyes are so hungry they could eat his hand. She wipes fat from the corners of her mouth with her hand-kerchief. In the morning light there's almost a moustache. They move me, those tiny blonde hairs, like an admission.

You must bring us your painting when it's finished, I say to her.

But I have finished it. It's out in the car, she says. She clatters out in her high heels. The gate creaks. The car door slams.

She's behind her painting, to prop it up. Her face is rosy, trembling.

What do you think? she asks.

Dad is silent.

Break it to me gently, she says.

Dad stares. To keep her pinned there, with the painting leaning on her.

At last he speaks.

The technique uses up a lot of paint.

Just like that. Nothing more. Technique. Uses up paint. It's a moment when time stretches, twists, somersaults, falls. She stands with her painting, waiting for him to say more. He's left the room, is screwing caps on tubes, has forgotten her. Below her armpits, she has no body, no noise, no laughter. The painting has robbed her of that, there's only a space down to her toes. Which are turned out, up-tipped, the leather scuffed, vulnerable. Above the painting her face is clumsy with Dad's derision.

I think: I'm like her.

I've painted here my pantheon, in a row like schoolyard figures fixed for a moment by the camera and choosing to look obedient. It's not a pantheon my father would've painted. He'd have put himself on that bench, with violence in his hands.

I've painted violence as a wanton schoolboy. And that's my father in the schoolboy's hands.

And from then on, the painting of the dance acquires a will of its own that engulfs me, although I fight. The brush refuses to paint the landscape and the figures Dad wants, it refuses to follow the original sketch, the painting no longer belongs to him or me. But it stays in my mind as no painting has ever done, when I'm not in front of the easel, when I'm peeling potatoes, washing dishes, putting out the garbage, I'm in the painting. The shape of the tea pot spout tells me to tuck more shadows in the faces, watching the cracking of an egg I decide to highlight leaves, the buttering of toast tells me to pin the sky straining to the top of the

canvas, taking clothes in from the line I know that the grass
in the foreground grows in spirals. The teapot, the egg, the
glittering butter, the soft sunny smell of clothes give me
answers, I go to the painting with certainty and the painting
resists. I battle against it, every day it's as formless as all
the other days. I must force my will on it, and every day
it's forcing its will on me. I achieve the evening exhausted
and lay down the brush and the next morning I find I've
achieved nothing. And then, capriciously, the left-hand
corner's right, and that spot in the sky's right and I sleep
soundly. And next morning, the spot in the sky and the
left-hand corner make senseless everything that's gone
before and I savage the yard with raking and wash out the
garbage bin in despair. But I'm comforted by the slow
furriness of a caterpillar and hurry inside to change the
whole canvas to suit the left-hand corner and the spot in
the sky. And I stop, spring clean the whole house, and when
the paint's dry discover that the spot in the sky and the left-
hand corner misled me, they're only paint. But now there's
the middle distance adept and alive, and I paint the whole
painting all over again in a panic because I know what I
should be doing, it'll be right at last, I must finish before
the knowledge recedes. And for days I cook elaborate
desserts and plan a new vegetable garden and sit in the
sunshine and then the canvas is dead. So I stare at it for
hours, days, I begin again, this time I know, I really know,
and I'm up to the third day and on the third day I know
nothing at all.

In exhaustion I lose my will power, and then the outlines
I'd made so determined to please Dad, the outlines rebel,
refuse to enclose. In terror I watch as under my brush everything on the canvas becomes part of everything else,
nothing keeps to its ordained place, chaos and uncertainty

are in the painting now and my exhausted body moves helplessly amongst shifting patterns.

It's getting a life of its own, says Molly. She's unbuttoning Dad's overcoat, carrying it away, her arms out in front of her, the coat across them like a supplication.

That's good, isn't it, she says. Still so eager, her mouth's open.

It must have a life of its own, says Dad, stiffly. So it can reflect on life.

But I'm a traveller with no map, foolish, a traveller with no language, layering paint on paint, filling in spaces that are no longer spaces, waiting, with the chaos whirling around. I have no struggle left in me, all I can do is wait, and who can do that better? The body reaches into the thickets and tangles of colour, it burrows into its own imagination, it disclaims a mere landscape, disclaims mere figures.

Those are hands, aren't they? says Molly, peering. Dancing hands. You've painted a picture of dancing hands.

And so *The Dance* is painted the way my imagination knows, it knows, my body knows, though I don't, I must learn and discover, and I find that in my cells is the knowledge of the shifting patterns of light, space, darkness, distance, all the glancing, meeting, parting of the dance, the sadness, the triumph, the hoping, having, losing of the dance between Dad and me, between me and the incandescent mystery, between me and The Gap. In a painting of hands.

It seems for me there's not a time when a painting's finished, only a time when I finish. When there's no struggle left in me, when a certain destination is reached but nothing is ended, when the paint hints that it could say everything but at the moment it won't.

I haven't reached that point yet.

That'll be enough, says Dad over my shoulder.

I'm squirting the day's paints on to the palette, the palette is full of possibilities while the colours are separate in their ordained order, compact, somewhere between passive and conscious, pent up.

I'm watching the painting, I'm dipping the brush in burnt umber, I'm almost at that finish, I stroke the canvas but in my happiness I'm sure this painting will never end, it's not finite this one and I'm inside its time, with my free hand I run my finger down from my forehead to just above my mouth, it's creating me, this painting, it's more than paint, more than me, the mystery promises to take place now and I'll be here, as yet insubstantial but here in the masses of colour, now, now, it's never happened before to me, after all this waiting it's happening, I won't breathe, eat, sleep, twitch, touch, scratch, think, if there's a God let it happen, let it happen now, it's breaking out of silence, it's yearning I can see, this is why I'm on earth for this moment, I must forget myself and let the brush, I shouldn't move the brush but I must, gently now gently and don't breathe, the caress into life or death, who cares, softly, softly, a wrong move, extend that line further, further, yes, no, that reduced it, not there damn it, not there but there, don't do that, you're trying to make meaning, let it tug gently of its own accord, let it come if it will, slowly, float on it, smooth and drown in it, gently, let it ease into life or death, it'll become, easy now.

Stop there, says Dad.

I hear the echo of his voice before I hear his voice. I remember where I am. This is the studio. The giant windows that command the world. The walls lit with morning. The pale sofa. The sink tinkling silver. The dressing-table crammed with pencils, tubes, crayons, rags, streaks of colour, pieces of paper, drawing pins, a ruler. This is my father at my back.

I'll take over now, he says.

I look at his face. He looks at the painting. I'm held by old habits, so I step aside. A small step onto other floorboards. I jostle Molly, she's standing where I move to, she must move back. I still have the brush streaked with burnt umber in my hand.

Dad's head is bowed, he's considering my palette, his lips twitch, he reaches over to the paint tubes, and selects Lamp Black. He squeezes Lamp Black onto the palette. Molly's breath on my neck is warm, then cool. This is how it happens, I say to myself as if I'm rehearsing how huge events happen. Just simple movements, a few steps, a voice, a nudge, a movement of the head, feet, fingers, the arm. The arm lifted. Nothing in the movements that portends. Just a man and his daughter. An artist and his amanuensis. The amanuensis was, after all, there for the artist. She was in the artist's studio, using the artist's brushes, his canvas, his colours, his techniques, she's breathing his air, living his life, painting his painting, she's him. She has no form, she's invisible.

He brings his arm down, he's changed his mind, he lays down one brush and picks up another. It's a long time since he's painted his own paintings, the old man with the loose lip, his hand fumbles around the brush handle, he's twirling it in Lamp Black, twirling, a fanfare of black.

Molly's arm is around my waist, there's a catch in her breathing, I don't look but I know the expression on her face, she's thinking of the old man with his trousers gathered around into his belt, of how he's returning to art, he'll paint again, he's beginning again. And the amanuensis, she must stand back, watch, elated as well. Must be pleased that her painting is not hers, has nothing to do with her, is his. Must be pleased that she's standing back here apart from the painting, watching, waiting again.

He's lowering his hand. He's uncertain of the brush. It has, after all, been twenty years since he held a brush. I've been his amanuensis twenty years. And only now have I given him the painting he really wanted. He has a right. All the right there is.

I will soon be asked to make a cup of tea. And must turn the teacup so the handle is on the right side, must cut the cake so it's the right size for his old man's mouth, must lower my eyes.

He's still fumbling his grip on the brush. Molly presses my waist, I'm angry at the bruises she's making on my skin.

I'd liked to have painted the story of a woman who spoke, who acted when the voice inside her whispered. I would've liked to have painted that I took action when my father claimed my painting as his own, I would've liked to have shown how I moved forward, Molly and my father quivering as I dashed the brush from his fingers, how his hand trembled in its sudden emptiness, how his eyes amidst their dreaming became points of light. How, when my father held out his hand to take the brush, I stood my ground, my back to the painting protecting it, my arms outstretched, how I shouted, let me tell you I would've liked to have painted myself shouting no, no, I couldn't permit him, I was not to be painted out, I could no longer live with this sense of death, something of all this belonged to me.

That's what I would've liked to have painted.

But I couldn't.

*

I turn, walk the length of the studio past the sofa, the paintings turned to the wall, the sink, I walk quietly so his concentration won't be disturbed, I go down the stairs quietly, I make tea, I cut cake, I set the tray. The only protest is the jangle of a teaspoon dropped on the lino. As I bend to pick it up, the door of a cupboard fills my vision. The cupboard near the stove. My eyes rest on the door. Then I straighten, get a clean teaspoon, carry the tray up the stairs.

He's not using the brush, he's using the palette knife. He's holding the knife firmly as he cuts through the oils. He brings the knife down in a diagonal, and across. He harvests my images with his knife. His hands fumble on a brush but they're strong on a knife.

Molly turns at my tread, her face is that expression before a question, when the face muscles pull at understanding. I bend, watch my feet, I'm careful with the tray. She helps me set out the tea things. When our fingers touch, it may mean nothing. I decide it means nothing. Because I'm finding what's inevitable in me.

That night, I kneel before the open cupboard doors, priming them. I've stolen whole tubes this time, not scrapings of palettes, not ends of tubes or bits squeezed out, I've stolen his paints, and there are many doors primed. If I'd looked up from the teacups at Molly, what would I have seen? The compressed lips of complicity, the sigh held under the breath that I'd be invited to echo. Felt compelled to echo. Afterwards, we'd have rattled teacups in the sink suds together, and hung tea-towels out to dry in the sun. A simple action, another one, that might have changed everything.

Now when I paint as his amanuensis on new paintings, Dad hovers. Too muddy, he says of my mixture of yellow and green. Put your darks in first, how long have I told you, he says. Bring in the background early so it's part of the picture.

His face is gashed by teeth.

So I clarify and put darks in and paint the background. But he won't go for walks with Molly, he won't even sit on the sofa. His hand when he wrenches the brush from me could strangle. I nod, swallow, gaze when he speaks. I say, now I understand, yes, yes, I see what you mean. Of course that's how it should be.

I even try: silly me.

A wrong note.

You defy me, you've always defied me, he says. That's been the fault in my work. Your defiance.

I put the brush down, move away from the painting to seem less possessive of it. I sit on the sofa so he's taller than me. The painting, barely begun, flares.

Molly comes in, and smiles. Artistic temperament, she explains.

Shut up, he roars at her.

But he paints quietly for a while. His arms move easily. The oils soothe.

We're running out of several colours. We're getting through them fast, he says.

I'll go to town, buy some immediately, says Molly.

I go downstairs, make another pot of tea. I've carried this tray up the stairs all my life. Watched the steam blur patterns of leaves in the windows.

This tea's so strong it could eat holes in the stomach, says Dad.

I've made tea like this all my life. Thousands maybe millions of spoonfuls of leaves from the jar with the green bubbles in the glass. The boiling water streaming down a lifetime.

I'll make another pot, I say.

Have mine, says Molly to him. She exchanges cups with him, plonking his on the tabletop in a way that usually makes him smile. She eases him, smooths down the edges, the way she moves cups. She's found her place. Our teeth click on the cake.

It should end there, the noise, the hate. But I find a resistance in me, he's right, there's always been a resistance in me. It's my visibility. The more I prime cupboard doors, the more insistent it is. A kind of violence.

Don't I have any say, I ask. Any rights?

Rights! he says. What are you talking about? Who do you think you are? This isn't a collaboration.

Teacups jump in their saucers. Molly's mouth at me is aggrieved.

He's knocking his chest with a clenched fist, as if he'd break himself in two to prove.

I am the artist, he's shouting. I am. And you ...

His hand dismisses me, I'm lighter than dust in the air ... You are the amanuensis. That's all.

He's out of his chair, bent over me with a finger.

And remember, anybody, anybody at all could be the amanuensis.

He pauses.

Molly misjudges for once. How's the tea now? she says.

Even Molly here. Molly could be my amanuensis. The amanuensis is entirely expendable, he shouts.

He stops, sits down. Molly stirs sugar loudly into his cup. But having begun, I must continue, though my bowels quake.

What about *The Dance*? I say.

Not all of Molly's frantic stirring can drown the silence.

What about *The Dance*? he says.

There you go, all sugared, she cries, making the spoon ring on the saucer.

If I could hold onto the sounds she makes, the ringing, stirring, rustling, the jolly cries, if they were solid, actual, a rope of sound that could tug me out of my submission.

I saw your face, he says. You tried to take the painting over, but you couldn't, it's mine, you, it, everything you know is mine, without me you don't exist. And that painting, every stroke on it is mine. My conception, my execution. I ordered. You obeyed. *The Dance* is more utterly mine than anything I've painted in my whole life. And never let me hear you try to claim it for yourself. It's my great work, at last.

The Dance, I notice a few days later, has been hidden behind the sofa. And a few weeks later, removed. Molly has put it in a competition in Sydney. She tells me this as I pull at weeds.

Why? I ask. Dad wants to be cut off from the world.

She prises up a weed. That's just his mask, she says. You must learn how to manage him. You always do things, take things, so, so excessively.

You're getting dirt under your fingernails, I say. You're not here to get dirt under your fingernails.

She doesn't walk away on a garden path, she swishes. Though Dad's confiscated her plastic mac, even her new demure clothes make noise. We understand each other, Molly and me. Almost. At another time I could love her. But now is always too precarious, always hurtling. And there are paintings she might see, demand to know the whole, expect that there is a whole, as Tim did. A totality.

Molly comes rushing in to show me the news in a paper she's driven to the shops to buy. *The Dance* has won the Biennale Prize.

The Lonely Visionary, it says, she reads. Isn't that just him?

She sees my face. You're a lonely visionary too, she says.

We ought to do something to mark the occasion, she adds. That's what normal people would do. Even artists.

I've been washing the windows, those giant eyes.

Are you disappointed? I ask.

In art? says Molly.

Yes, I say, after a pause.

The rag's dripping, says Molly.

She helps with the smears. We're two tiny women flailing the glossy surfaces.

It's the way art's made, says Molly. That's what's disappointing. The makers have no grandeur. Only their works.

Dad refuses any festivities.

But admit you're thrilled, says Molly.

I'm furious, says Dad. That they've taken this long to notice me again.

He turns to me.

There are runs on the glass, he says.

Over dinner he swallows large chunks of meat, he's too impatient to use his knife.

From now on, he says, we'll do things differently.

Two chunks go into his mouth at once. I watch his throat distend.

A vision transfigures the inner life, he says. Spatial relationships, colour, perspectives, these are symbols in a visionary's private world. The visionary has a private knowledge of truth.

Now I know, it falls around me like light, that he doesn't pull his words out of an incandescence. He probably reads them in his books he won't let me open, and rehearses his phrases as he walks on the road. Daily he's considered my captivity, my enchantment.

A private truth, says Molly. Can truth be private?

Molly's mouth moves over his words. She's reciting them to herself in delight, so she'll remember them while she's cleaning her teeth, standing in a queue, tying a knot in a shoelace. As I have always done.

Far too private to share, he continues. Besides, Frances, you need to pay more attention to the house. This meat, for instance. You obviously gave no thought to its preparation.

He spits it out. Those loose lips, they can hurl meat. It hits the wall.

It's a wonder it didn't break the plaster, he says. Just concentrate on the house, that's your job. From now on, I'll paint alone.

I'm standing. And though my voice is croaking, I say it.

And I'll paint on my own.

Over my dead body, he says.

I stand at night in front of the opened cupboard doors in the kitchen. The whispers in Dad's house, the flurries, they tell me what I love, what's part of me, what's not. I stand at night with the treasure of stolen paints, and on my brush they swirl together like whispers. There are many cupboard doors, the insides of doors, the outsides, these are my canvases, the main kitchen, the main bathroom, the laundry, the hall, my bedroom, my parents' bedroom.

I know at last my life's purpose. To paint the absorbed history of my waiting. My imagination, my body knows it all, its intricate and precise machinations. Every night I listen to voices inside me, I let them paint, I'm full of voices. I find my hands painting girls at school, women in shops, delivery boys, a child who smiled, boys in a dark garden shed, a minister framed by rain and roses, a wedding dress trailing on a blue carpet, a coffin gold with flames, rumours of distant revolutions, the hubbub of years, of my waiting.

My purpose is the rooms of Dad's house. To put patterns of paint everywhere. And one day, to paint them all over his studio.

I paint pictures through the secrets of night, every night, every surface. I sleep little, to prevent dreams.

Your eyes are shining strangely, says Dad a few months later as I take the salt and pepper from the table.

This time off painting is doing her good, says Molly. Though the housework must be a burden. We should share it.

Dad gets up and leaves her sitting framed by an empty window. I hurry downstairs.

There are the walls, the ceilings. So many surfaces. While I make their bed, I think of more. The broom cupboard. I've overlooked the broom cupboard. And the cranny where the trays go. I should have a plan. Something to judge and consider. On a piece of paper, to lie on a table while I cut cabbage.

But I'm as pent up as any whorl of vermilion on a palette.

I bolt my food to hurry Dad and Molly, if I can get them to finish three minutes earlier than usual, that's three minutes more to paint. After all those years, I know how long three minutes is.

I steal his tubes of paint with joy. I become fastidious about his dressing-table, moving tubes, jars, bottles, bits of rag to confuse.

I can't find anything these days, he says.

But it looks much neater, says Molly. She's putting her heart and soul into organising you.

In my haste, I become careless.

There's paint in the lines of your fingers, Dad says.

I look down, my fingers are traitors, they could leave emerald marks on skin.

It's that big clean up she did, says Molly. Such a messy job. And isn't your work better for a bit of order?

I don't baulk at ceilings. Though the creak in my neck gets worse, I make ladders from tables, chairs, chairs on chairs. Once, a pyramid topples but my fall is light. Bouncing on the balls of my feet, I laugh at my own lightness and the rush of air.

Strange, that when you reach into the mystery at last, it no longer seems like God. Later, people insist: Your limbs, body, mind—you must've been transparent with wonder; surely you looked around, surely you can tell me. But I can't. I was there, but too busy to see. I only looked at my painting.

So it also remains an undiscovered country and no traveller returns with tales.

I thought I heard something crash last night, says Molly.

Molly, I can see, insists on knowing. Her cheeks are hollows.

Nothing happened, I say. I'm like a balloon in my private joy but tethered by fear.

Probably it was the neighbours, I think to add. They've built those townhouses so close.

I baulk at my parents' bedroom. The door has been shut since Auntie shut it. I double back, find other spaces for pictures. I paint pictures within pictures. On the backs and underneaths of the china cabinet, the kitchen table, the kitchen chairs, their legs. On the hallstand. The grandfather clock. On china, on vases. On my bedhead, bedbase. I find I've overlooked the inside of drawers. And the sections of floor where I don't often walk. But everything will finally lead back to the door of my parents' bedroom.

I'm painting, I know, in a frenzy. The paint argues with me. I work against its argument. It says: you have no right. I argue back, timid, determined. I say: I am painting to save my life.

One day Dad will hear us argue, the paint and I. Certain things are inevitable.

Like their bedroom door. For a month, I put away the paints. Go for long walks on the concrete paths where the scrub once was. Sit with Molly, let her talk to me about the husband she once had, the children, the house.

Go into the township, look at the fruit in the green-grocer's window arranged in patterns, sunbursts of bananas on a green apple sky. Buy a small carton of milk in a shop.

Just that one little carton? asks the woman. Our mouths open together when I start to answer. I look at her, at the shop fridge behind her with its wet panes of glass, at the round-shouldered cash register stuck with little paper reminders of today and yesterday.

There's no family? she asks.

No family, I say.

Her mouth's still open like a crying baby's, in an infinity sign.

There is, however, a father, I say.

Ah, she says. Her mouth closes. A father.

I walk slowly out of the township easy at the intersections so the youths with Walkmans don't notice my difficulty at the kerbs. I watch a neon sign in the sky above a gymnasium say SQUASH like an instruction or a revelation. But a light bulb on the curl of the Q pops and defects.

I borrow money from Molly I'll never pay back and take a taxi to Kookaburra. I get out fifty metres down the road, ask the driver to wait. He switches the radio on, an advertising jingle blows tatters of sound past the ageing woman lingering by a tree trunk. A teenage boy comes out of a back shed, picks his teeth, glances at the taxi, goes back inside. His face is, is not like Tim's, my heart's thumping too fiercely to judge. The driver beeps. I knock on the door of the house softly, hoping no-one will come, I knock loudly, demanding someone come. I drag myself across stiff grey weeds to the shed, knock on wood that swings away from its nail. The boy sticks his head out the door. I gaze.

What do you want? he asks after a while.

I don't know, I answer after a while.

As we do a U-turn in the taxi, the boy's still watching, his hands sticking straight out from his body, and only a hammer to hold in them.

In the taxi, I remember making love. Say the word, say it. They all do these days. It's even written on the bus stop seats. Fucking. I demanded an epiphany from Tim, I remember. It was coded in the word we used. Make love. Create love. It seemed a way to become like Dad.

I open the door of my parents' bedroom.

Everything protects against truth. It's difficult to pass through certain door frames. I stand at the threshold, stare at the wood. It's pitted, worn, like the wood of old wharves.

I carry in a jangle of mop, mop bucket, broom, dustpan. The noise rears against the air, dusty through yellowed slats of venetian blinds that won't open. I clean. Then I peer at the dirt in the dustpan, on the broom bristles, on the mop, in the swill of mop water. It's only dirt.

But the room has its own time which cannot be reduced by a swill of mop water. Its own imperative.

Sometime late in the day, or night, I reach the wardrobe. Newspaper clippings crackle under the wardrobe, cocooned in shadows. Is Mum's skin like this, forty odd years later? Or has it shrivelled off the bones? The mysterious smile on the skeleton. Things happen so quickly in the grave. Whereas living is very long. Just a few events to pierce holes in the darkness. Menstruation. Almost a wedding. A death that no-one noticed. Perhaps it was before the wedding. Making love. Painting with my father. Here's a ball-dress, tattered by moths, unravelling, falling light as ashes.

But I move towards what's inevitable. I feel further under the wardrobe for the obstruction that's always been there, that I've known about since Mum, that I've never pulled out into the light. A sharp-edged board, I turn it over and find I'm looking at a painting in oils on masonite. It's a portrait of a man, surely it's Dad, this is the way his eyes fit into their sockets, the way his eyebrows rise into the forehead, his lips flare like these, and that's his squared jaw. But something's amiss, it's as if he's been looking at himself in the reflections on rippling water that tell lies, or truths. His eyes, which have always seemed to hold such secrets, the brush has made them slide away, calculating who's watching, and his jaw, arched in determination, no, the brush discovers, no, that's not it at all, that jaw is arched in blind arrogance and those cheeks, they balloon like a clown's, and the mouth sneers.

I stay where I am on my knees in the long silence of my parents' bedroom, I turn the masonite over as if the hatching on the back could offer clues, I turn it round again, wipe the cobwebs from the corners, trace with my fingers the paths of the brush, once so exploratory, now with time solidified, oracular. It's a mean, dishonest, ignorant face. A face that knows nothing.

And I think of Dad, I think of his face, I've examined every bone, muscle, pore of it, I've watched it all my life and now I admit that this is the face I've known, but never seen. And he's always seen it, he must have, to paint a self-portrait like this.

A long, long while after, I put the painting down. The eyes stare at the ceiling, calculating. I turn the portrait face down on the carpet. And remember the newspaper clippings.

The newsprint is thick and black and cryptic with authority. The words on its soft creases become powder on my fingers but fragments reveal totalities.

Here are the walls I've moved between most of my life, the bedroom of my parents, my bedroom, the hall, the kitchen, the bathroom, the laundry. Out there the stairs, up there his studio. All I need to do is dissolve into them. Here's my bed, the acquiescent sheets, my chest moving of its own accord up and down, the heart continuing to beat. All I need to do is dissolve. The Gap, the blessed Gap, nothing.

But every now and then a thought intrudes, trembles in The Gap, palpitates. I think: that's the swish of a broom. I think: I'm holding the broom, I must be sweeping. I think: I'll destroy him and all his paintings. I think: I can't do that to my father, whoever he is. I think: there are eggs boiling in an effervescence of steam. I think: I must be boiling eggs. I think: that painting, he painted this terrible truth, it's not a ruse, he knows what he is.

Molly's face looms, connected to the ceiling.

You've taken to your bed a lot. Are you sick?

I turn to the wall, dissolve into The Gap.

Violence for Art's Sake

SYDNEY. THURS. After several weeks
of court hearings a man was
acquitted of a charge of murder of his
wife. The man, an established
artist, had been held in custody pend-
ing Police investigations of

said that it is all very well to condemn
such behaviour, but allow-
ance must be made for the

by the magnificence of his talent and
by birthright an inheritor and
maker of a firmament of greatness.
Our civilization depends on his
like. It has been rightly said that
while man might be sacred, his
condition isn't. If the circumstances

terrible means. It deserves not soci-
ety's condemnation but its
compassion. War teaches us that we
may have to use violence to bring
peace. The defendant may have
had to apply this reasoning

Such an accident could happen to
any man at the moment of passion,
said Justice Sorenson, in a summing

The coroner reported that there
was substantial bruising around the
throat. The oesophagus showed signs
of severe contrusions and the
larynx had been crushed. Massive
and prolonged force had been exerted
on the woman by the application of
extreme manual pressure consistent
with the act of strangulation.

I find myself in the pantry, cleaning shelves, in the laundry, water slopping round my elbows, at the washing line, pegging clothes. I watch myself clean shelves, wash, peg clothes. These are the rhythms that comfort. That postpone.

But one morning, I go into the backyard. It's that blur of dawn when the air holds immobility like stones do. Not enough light for shadows under the peelings of bark, not enough life for veined leaves to burrow into earth, no sudden spurting of colour as the bottle brush fights against the grey garden. I think: my mind is clear.

A bird calls, a cry like a mournful child. I think: something must be done. Done by me.

I walk to where the old hen house was, past the bare patch in the lawn where Dad burnt his pictures. After all these years the grass still knows, it hasn't forgotten. There was a gate here, swinging with yellow dandelions where I vowed never to be like Mum, as easily as crossing my heart and hoping to die. Grit was, I remember, noisy against my teeth.

I'm looking back to my father's house. It is, after all, quite small. And top heavy with his studio. Almost the lower bricks stagger to carry the weight. There's a jagged line along the length of each brick and rising to the brick above. As if the house might yawn open. There was a moment in my childhood when my father's house, its roof, windows, doors, foundations, all turned and twisted towards a vanishing point in obedience to my father's words, everything in a grand and precise procession. In this light, the mountains, once majestic with his thoughts, slump. The land all around me was once shadowy with Dad's knowledge. Now there are no craggy secret places, no places to hide. The leaves once seemed arranged for his thoughts. But now I see that they are strewn only in random on the ground. The very dirt which seemed to whisper what Dad knew, glints between my fingers only because of the slow grinding of many rocks. The path leads to the gate leads to the road leads to a suburban shopping centre, to other suburbs, cities, to the sea, to other countries, back to here. Only to here. The dull sky, the clumps of weeds, the straggling trees, nothing, nothing is arranged to the glory of my father.

And I have been waiting all my life. The cold ground presses scornfully against my heels. And now I can hate.

I'm running inside, banging doors, finding matches, scooping the newspaper clippings from my parents' room, finding more newspaper, finding twigs. The bare patch will be good for another fire. No, the bare patch is too far from the house. My hands shaking, dropping matches on the frosty grass. Kerosene. I remember the slop of kerosene in his studio. There's kerosene in the laundry. Running, throwing open doors, another slop of kerosene. I look up at his detestable window, his detestable studio. And realise at last that I've never understood infinity. Oh, I heard his explanation, but I looked at his paintings. And his paintings said that everything, the whole world visible and invisible, magnificent and tawdry, everything, the path gleaming with new sunrise, the touch of a finger, the grating of a voice, even the reedy mockery of kookaburras now bursting out of a sleeping tree, everything converged ultimately in the eyes of my father. He was here, yet at that distant vanishing point. At infinity. All things met in him.

Only one painting disputed.

Molly comes rushing to my side as I swoosh kerosene.

No, she's shouting, arms struggling, her hands and mine fight for a tiny box of matches which the grass claims, dampens. Bruised by her eyes, her hands, I find one of the newspaper clippings. Screwed up into a ball. I rip it apart and the word's here on my fingers.

The word about my mother. My sad, my beautiful mother.

Strangulation.

Here, I shout. See. Acknowledge.

Dimly I hear a window slam. In the studio. In him. In me.

But Molly will not look. When I shove the newspaper in the new direction of her eyes, she turns her face the other way. No! she shouts. She grabs the matches, the kerosene, the hem of her dressing-gown and runs into the house. She locks the door against me and stands at the window.

I'm on the lawn and though the day slants with sunshine, I'm very cold. My feet are grey. I can't touch, rescue my mother. All I can do is twitch grey feet on frosty grass. After a while I signal to Molly through the window. She unlocks the door, lets me in, hands me a blanket, makes a pot of tea. We sit in the kitchen with all my paintings around us. They dance, these fragments, erratic in the morning light.

The fire, I say, was for my mother. And for me. Not that it would've solved anything.

I'm glad of the warmth of the blanket. I wrap it around my feet.

There is, I say, only one truthful painting by my father.

I go into my parents' bedroom, trailing the blanket. My feet patter on the kitchen lino. I carry back the painting of his face, his one moment. We breathe over it, Molly and I. I hear her heart still thumping. She pushes back a strand of hair.

Who did it? she asks.

What do you mean? I ask.

I stare at her strand of hair that falls wilfully back.

There's no signature on it, she says. It's funny that he didn't sign it. I wonder why.

He didn't sign it, I repeat.

The ordinary kitchen. The ordinary steam rising white from teacups. The woman frowsy in a dressing-gown, with tumbling hair. The question that becomes extraordinary.

I've never known him not to put his name on a painting, she's saying.

And my answer is cutting under her words.

My mother, I'm whispering. I think it was painted by my mother.

I touch my mother. Almost.

It's over here, the only painting on an easel, the only painting by my mother.

You spoke sir? It's a masterpiece, I heard you tell your wife.

A masterpiece stashed under a wardrobe for forty years, the only extant work of a young, unknown but brilliant artist, the victim of a cruel murder.

To me its greatest beauty is its poignancy. And the thing that comes trembling out of it—look, look, before it's too late, it's ephemeral, it's dying. Something, I think, like truth.

I don't go back up to his studio again, and he doesn't walk down the stairs and through the door. Molly brings me paints, brushes, charcoal, linseed oil, turps, pencils, clothes, palette knives, food, she stands and watches with arms folded, and goes quietly away. It takes a long time to paint pictures on the ceiling, walls, floor, the wardrobe in my parents' bedroom. While I paint on them, shadows lengthen and shorten, the air is chilly, warm, chilly, warm, light moves across the window panes and darkness too, planets rotate, seasons pass. But I keep painting. Now I don't paint about my life. I paint the death of my father.

I paint him at his windows, the windows that teeter on

those giant cliffs, he stands, a god, a sentinel, a ruse. I paint his face a hundred times, the face that knows only itself. I paint his muscles clenched, the lips silent, I paint the way he throws back his head to watch the canvas, the way he walks, his trenchancy. The way his eyes search only for his own thoughts beyond my shoulder. Most of all, I paint his hands, that can hold a brush or a neck, but his grip on the brush is gentle. I paint the landscape that he sees, shapes and distances grotesque with power, I paint the landscape that I see, and shiver. It may be that the room is cold. I paint the landscape through the days and nights. If the colours aren't true, they have their own truth. And then I come back to the wall where I've painted him at his windows, the windows that command.

Then I paint movements, simple movements, the creak on the floorboards behind him, his neck taut, the bones lifting the skin, he knows my step, the pressure of my hands, I paint the way he wouldn't look around to see me, the way he wouldn't bother to acknowledge me. I paint the way I'd push him through his windows, he wouldn't look around, the parabolas of glass would fall so gently, and he'd fall with them.

Do you think you ought? asks Molly, breaking a silence of weeks. You might put a hex on him.

I don't think people can, I say. And anyway, I have no wish to affect him. This isn't for him. It's for me.

I paint my violence into patterns, and that's how I contain it. If I couldn't paint, perhaps I'd have murdered him.

But there's more violence than mine in the world.

There's something wrong with his hands, Molly tells me one day. They're paralysed.

So I paint his hands falling down the cliff, emerald green in the whorls of skin, cerulean blue in the knots of knuckles, vermilion under the nails as they grasp at sandstone, which falls with him in a drift of gold.

And when he dies, and they carry him down the stairs, I open the stairs door to look, and his face is neither knowledgeable nor ignorant. He was just another person, but used by violence more than most.

I keep on painting.

I paint the story of my longing, my waiting, on the stairs and the stairwell wall and the stairwell ceiling and, step by step, at last I gain his studio. Molly moves out, against my persuasion.

Please stay, I say.

I love art, she says. But I can't stand the smell of it.

There's no time for sadness. In another lifetime, if there's one, I'll love well, Mum, Auntie, Molly and Tim. But now I must paint.

Though sometimes I forget where I am, I forget that I possess his studio at last and I start to think I'm painting on the wall, ceilings, floors, the secret crypts and vaulted heights of labyrinths, labyrinths within labyrinths, not just my own, but everyone who's spent their lives waiting, I hear them joining in, I hear the swishing of their brushes, millions of them, an orchestra of brushes, and my brush catches the melody of swishing and singing and sings with it too until I can't hear myself think and I have to stop and say: I'm in a house which is, after all, a smallish house, in a studio which is only a room, and all I'm doing is painting.

Ladies and gentlemen, I'll leave you alone with the exhibition.